TANGLED SHEETS

Stories & Poems of Lesbian Lust

EDITED BY
ROSAMUND ELWIN
KAREN X. TULCHINSKY

women's
PRESS

CANADIAN CATALOGUING IN PUBLICATION DATA

Tangled sheets: stories and poems of lesbian lust
ISBN 0-88961-207-2

1. Lesbians' writings, Canadian (English).* 2. Lesbians' writings, American. 3.
Erotic poetry, Canadian (English) — Women authors. 4. Erotic stories,
Canadian (English) — Women authors. 5. Erotic poetry, American — Women
authors. 6. Erotic stories, American — Women authors. 7. Lesbianism —
Poetry. 8. Lesbianism — Fiction. 9. Canadian poetry (English) — 20th century.*
10. Canadian fiction (English) — 20th century.* 11. American poetry — 20th
century. 12. American fiction — 20th century. I. Elwin, Rosamund, 1955-
II. Tulchinsky, Karen X.

PS8235.L47T35 1995   C810.8'03538   C95-931328-1
PR9194.5.L47T35 1995

CREDITS:
Sailor by Gerry Gomez Pearlberg was previously published in *Long Shot*'s Fall
1993 issue.
Hold Me Down and *I Bought A New Red* by Chrystos is reprinted from *In Her
I Am* (Press Gang, 1993) by permission of the author and the publisher.
Edmonton by Kiss & Tell is reprinted from *Her Tongue on My Theory* (Press
Gang, 1993) by permission of the author and the publisher.
The Old Fashioned Way by Lucy Jane Bledsoe and *True Story* by Eve Harris
were first published in *On Our Backs*.
Please Wear Romantic Attire first appeared in *Leatherwomen II*, edited by
Laura Antoniou, Rosebud, 1994.
Night on the Town © copyright 1995 Lesléa Newman previously appeared in
The Femme Mystique also © copyright 1995 Lesléa Newman (Alyson
Publications) and is reprinted by permission of the author.

Cover photograph: Dianne Whelan
Cover design: Sandra Haar (with thanks to Jacqueline Rabazo Lopez for the last
minute technical assistance)
Editor: Michele Paulse
Photograph of editors: Dianne Whelan

Published by Women's Press, Suite 233, 517 College Street, Toronto, Ontario,
Canada M6G 4A2.

This book was produced by the collective effort of Women's Press.
Women's Press gratefully acknowledges the financial support of
the Canada Council and the Ontario Arts Council.

Printed and bound in Canada
1 2 3 4 5 1999 1998 1997 1996 1995

CONTENTS

POEMS

INTRODUCTION

Tangled Sheets is about lesbian sex. All kinds of lesbian sex. Some pieces in this collection are written in explicit language and are hot, passionate and raw. Others are sensuous, romantic and sweet.

When we posted the call for submissions for this anthology we posed the question, "Do lesbians fuck?" We asked for stories and poems about lesbian sex. We wanted to know what women do in bed with each other. We dared lesbians to tell it all. And we received many brave revelations.

Tangled Sheets encompasses stories of women of various ages, cultural, class and physical backgrounds. The pieces in this collection represent a range of experiences by a diverse mix of writers — established and emerging — from Canada and the United States. Given that desire is subjective and recognizing that what makes one lesbian hot, bores another, what offends one lesbian turns another on, selecting the stories and poems for this anthology was difficult.

Tangled Sheets is another addition to the growing body of lesbian sex literature. It is a sequel to *Getting Wet: Tales of Lesbian Seductions*. The great response *Getting Wet* continues to receive reassures us that lesbians want to read about lesbian sex written in language, set in places and occurring in circumstances we can relate to.

We have structured the anthology to allow stories to immediately follow one another, telling varied tales of lesbian desire. The poems slide from one to the other, much like the subtle and sexy dance of seduction which occurs between women.

We encourage all lesbians, not just those whose work appears here, to continue to write and submit their work for future anthologies. Our printed voices are important. Anthologies such as this one document and demystify lesbian sex, and, of course, are a continued source of enjoyment to lesbians.

Tangled Sheets will excite, entice, entertain and seduce women who love and have sex with other women. We want lesbians to find *Tangled Sheets* the morning after an especially hot night, tangled in discarded clothes and sheets, haphazardly tossed on the floor during a passionate moment the evening before.

We'd like to acknowledge the work of Dionne Falconer, who began this project as a co-editor and helped to get it under way — thanks Dionne.

Rosamund Elwin   *Karen X. Tulchinsky*

Tangled Sheets

Stories

SANDRA HAAR/ELLEN FLANDERS

All for You

Slowly she starts to touch herself. I reach out but she shoves my hand away. "Don't even think of touching me. I want you so frustrated it hurts." I knew she would say that. Still, I receive it as a fresh realization. I moan softly and plead with her: "I've been aching. I want it so badly. Please." I say it pathetically.

She just smiles slyly, gets off the bed, and heads towards the closet. I groan with anticipation. My cunt is throbbing, heavy and swollen. When she reappears, she's decked out in stiletto boots, with a zipper up the back, stockings and the leather garter I had bought for her earlier that day. Her tits are squeezed into a leather bustier, slightly unzipped. She is spilling over the top.

I watch her like a hungry schoolboy or a dirty old man in a porn theatre. I can't touch myself so I squirm and look like an idiot trying to get myself off. I know this display of frustration pleases her, encouraging the performance. My attention is crucial. She rubs her cunt and spreads her lips to show me how wet she is. This, too, is crucial. She's inches from my face and I can smell her. I reach out with my tongue hoping she will brush over it. Not yet. She holds my head back with one hand and rubs her cunt with the other. I'm rubbing myself on the bed, drooling. My muscles strain and ache. I'm going nowhere.

Lying on the floor she swings her legs around in the air, opening and closing them like I've seen strippers do. She rolls onto her stomach and raises her ass spreading her cheeks and cunt for me to see the cum drip onto the carpet. She does it for me. I see her fingering herself and playing with her asshole. I want her to sit on my face and rub her cum all over my nose and mouth, to use me to wipe herself, to use me. I want my nose to be buried in her ass and be forced to smell her while she plays with her cunt. I want to be used and wanted; reduced and released. She does it for me and I return the favour.

"I want to fuck myself. I want to stuff your big dick in my cunt." She grabs me by the hair, lifts my head until I am straining upwards. "Is this yours?" she asks, waving my cock under my nose. "Is it?" I nod. It has to be. She tells me to get my dick wet and ready for her. She tells me to get it nice and slick, pushing my head downwards. Then pulls me up and pushes me down 'til I choke. She pulls the cock out of my mouth, takes it away from me. She fucks herself slowly at first, intent on giving me a show. When my attention is no longer necessary, she focuses on orgasm. Drooling, I watch, humping the bed like a dog in heat. She groans as she cums. I groan too.

I'm on my stomach in the bathroom with her fist up my cunt. She's fucking me hard, telling me to come for her and I'm thanking her for it.

This is not the only way it happened.

I look good and knowing it makes me look even better. It gets me what I want and I'm getting turned on. The height of my heels, the precariousness but also the power of striding in these boots, the tautness of the muscles in my thighs and calves. Every piece produces its own sensation; has its own function. A leather garter stretching across my ass holds up stockings tight around my thighs. The bustier pushing my tits up and tight against my rib-cage.

From behind, the garter frames me like an archway. As I turn to face her, it barely reveals my pussy. Moving from there, she can see the swell of my breasts. Across my upper chest to a strongly muscled neck, softly rounded muscles on my upper arms, expressive face with dark eyes and a slick, deep-red, lipsticked mouth.

I like being effective. I like being in control of every element. The zipper precisely halfway down the bustier, the laces on my garter spreading as they go toward the crack of my ass. Control adds tension to the taut string of desire. I am not slack. I am determined. I am risking a lot and I don't intend to lose.

I stand in front of the bed, my hands first covering then pulling back the hair to reveal my pussy, pulling my lips back to reveal the red. She is watching me, her stomach flat against the mattress. She won't touch herself. I know that, I told her not to. I like to see her growing desire. It makes her hungrier. And a better spectator. I like to see the effect I'm having. The tension between wanting to look and then looking becomes unbearable. I open my pussy lips, push my ass out and open my pussy from behind. Down on my knees, I slide my finger into my cunt and draw the juice out. To show more, to show less, slowly, this is what I'm doing.

To command attention, not to lose it, this is what I'm riding on.

It's hard for her and I can empathize. There are things I want so much I can't even think what they are, but all the same, right now, it's me who decides what to give and how much. Thinking about what is to happen next, I orgasm, pushing her cock deep inside, pressing my engorged clit against my pubic bone.

Her face hits the cold bathroom tiles. My spike heels make a sharp clicking noise against them. Her body is trembling and in need. I fulfil that need. I mean to be effective. I give her as much as she can take and only a little bit more. Her pussy engulfs my fist and she pushes her body back against me. She comes in a frenzied blur of sweat and pussy fluids.

I realize that I, too, am drenched. I unzip my boots and unsnap the garters. I draw her against me and kiss her. I grin. She grins, too.

This is not the only way it happened.

CATHERINE CREEDE

Double Vision

There's a secret, lurking little fantasy that I have. My lover knows about it, but I've always been afraid I'd be drummed out of the dyke league if I talked about it out loud. That is, out loud to anyone except my lover, my dear sweet Nat, the love of my life, warm full presence in my bed, possessor of the voice that lifts me up beyond the now, throws me into the world she creates with me with her words, her whispers, her shouts. She knows about this fantasy, she encourages it, she starts it with me...and, like me, she wonders where it comes from, where it's going. We analyze it — queer kind of dykes we are, fantasizing about boys — but not to death.

Oh yes, it's still very much alive, there between us, as much a part of our repertoire of sex toys as her blue jeans, the drawer full of dildos and butt plugs, our vibrator that we use (and the battery-powered useless one we can't throw away, because it was the first one she ever bought me, and she was so cute about it), lube, condoms and a medical sized box of gloves. Sometimes, the morning after we've had a fight, when I empty the wastebasket in our bedroom, I see the layers of our life and connection, a dig of layers, latex, then kleenex, then more latex. Tears and love, tears and lust, layered together in the safety of our bed.

My fantasy...is part of my reality. My fantasy is this sweet strong woman, my lover, in control, fucking a man who looks like her, making him want it. I vary it...but that part is always the same. Usually, I'm there, encouraging her, making her want it. I'm the one sitting, she's watching me sitting and watching, he's not paying attention to me, he's watching her. We're all in a dyke bar and my Nat is in her jeans, her docs, a white cotton shirt, her black leather jacket. I'm sitting at a table, watching. Across from me is a man I've barely noticed, except to note that he looks remarkably like Nat — the same carved features and short dark hair, even the same jeans and jacket.

It's dark, crowded, noisy. The crowd absorbs the edge of the noise. The music is in us, and Nat's dancing to a slow and grinding, saxophone-smoky piece of music that yanks and pulls at my clit, music I get wet listening to.

Nat's dancing, her hips moving, her ass tightening as she barely moves to the music, and she moves over to me, gets me up out of my chair, dances me against the wall, grinding into my ass with the music, placing her hands around my hips and holding me against her, knowing how wet I am, how hard my clit is from watching her, from Margo Timmins' "Sweet Jane," whispered and ground out and reaching at my gut.

Nat leans forward, still grinding, still dancing, and I'm completely still, pressed against the wall, silent, my eyes closed, wanting, pressing my nipples against the cold wall because I need friction, I need to be touched, I need her to suck them. I want her, I reach my arm around behind me and try to cup my fingers between her legs, around her hips, but she holds me too tightly. Her lips are on my neck and she whispers to me, reminding me we're in a public place. I feel her breath against my neck, the flicker of her soft warm alive tongue on my earlobe, a brief, hot, tight nip on my ear. "You know I want to fuck you. I want to take those clothes off you, I want to pinch and suck those tits that want me so much. I know you want me, I can feel how hard your tits are, I know your cunt is wet and hard. You need to be touched. But I'm not going to fuck you here. You're going to have to wait. And it's going to be a long wait. Before you get fucked, you're going to have to watch me with someone else."

She snakes her arm between my body and the wall and suddenly pinches my right nipple, hard, holding it as I cry out, wanting, and she presses herself even more closely against me. "You know what I'm going to do, don't you?" Her voice is low and fierce, ripping at me as she kneads my nipple between her fingers and I'm voiceless against the wall. "You know what I'm going to do — you saw that guy, the one who's watching us, I'm going to take him home with us and fuck him, and you're going to watch. I'm going to make him want, and tease him until he doesn't know what the hell hit him, and you're going to watch. You like that, don't you? You like to think about me getting fucked by a man, you like to think about me opening my wet butch cunt for a hard dick, a hard dick that only I can let in, a dick that I have control over, you like that don't you?"

I nod, breathless against the wall, breathless at her words, her hands against me. I see the man watching, I see his mouth tight, his shoulders and muscles tensed, his hand working itself tightly into a fist, loosening, tightening again as he watches, as he sees. I watch him watching us, knowing he wants her, knowing he sees our want, but not knowing he's part of it. His arousal is high and loud, breathless and suspended, taut, the muscles of his thighs powerful and tight and clenched. He lowers his hand beneath the table and I see him stroke himself surreptitiously, furtively. He doesn't look down, he keeps his gaze on us, his eyes slightly downcast so that we can't look straight into them. He clearly wants, he can't help but touch his visibly hard cock, but he keeps biting his lip, barely controlling his arousal.

Watching him, I feel Nat's breath on my neck, her hand circling my nipple, pinching touching kneading her cunt pressed against my ass circling in sync with her hand on my tit and I let a slight moan escape. Her knowing fingertips tighten on my nipple, pinch hard — "Shhhh." She grabs around the outside of my hips, digging her fingertips slightly into the flesh beneath the bone and grinds closer. "Quiet. No noises. Shut up. Or you don't get to watch me fuck him. You see him want me — but you have to cooperate, you have to do what I say. Or I won't let you watch. I'll make you listen, and I'll cuff your hands so you can't touch yourself while you're listening." She continues grinding into my ass, holding me against her with her hips. The music is still smoky, still Margo, still inside my gut, my cunt, my wanting.

In sync and in rhythm to Margo, Nat dances her fingertips down my thighs and gently lets me go, moving naturally and lightly, without calling much attention to her movements, over to the table where he sits. Stunningly, surprisingly, no one seems to have noticed this exchange which is taking place much more quickly than I can believe. I am left leaning face against the cold wall, my cunt thick and wet and wanting, the seams of my jeans pressed against my hard open clit. Even inside my jeans I feel myself open.

I lean, recovering, watching my lover with the man who mirrors her. She's sitting now against a chair backwards, the chair tucked easily under her sprawled legs. I know she's sitting so her clit is pressed against the chair, so the hard wetness created by her dance with me is stroked, pulsed. She looks so calm, so together, so casual next to the tension of the man she's now leaning over to talk to. As she gently puts her hand on his thigh, he leans back and closes his eyes, and even from where I am, I hear his sharp intake of breath as she begins to knead the flesh around his knee. She takes his hand and gently pulls him to his feet. He rises to meet her height, to reflect her in reverse, the wanting masculine counterpoint to her butch controlled restraint.

Almost tenderly, she leads him from the bar by propelling him ahead of her, her hand on the small of his back. He walks quietly, silently, content and waiting for her signals. I am almost fooled into thinking they are a couple, they look so much alike, he seems to trust her so much, until she pauses in a slightly darkened corner near the door in the shadow of the coats, and backs him against the wall. From the distance I'm following them at I can see his half-closed eyes, his chest tight, his nipples outlined hard through his white t-shirt. Nat stands in front of him, barely touching, circling her hands around the outside of his nipples, pausing suddenly to pinch first one then the other in quick succession. The sharp pain drives his obvious arousal one step further and he sags back against the wall, desire and wanting and questioning tightening in his lean sculpted body. Nat takes him by the shoulders and turns him around to face the wall and covers his back with her body. I see her slide her hand around the front and I know without having to see it that she's stroking his hard cock outside his jeans, fully, tightly. She strokes and pulls and kneads with her right hand, her other hand holding his ass tightly against her by his hip. She rubs him for a moment too long, it seems to me, as I stand leaning against the wall, feeling what they're doing rather than seeing it in the shadows, my own tits and clit and wet cunt responding to the movements I sense Nat doing to him. I feel her rubbing his cock, I feel myself as the owner of the cock, wanting her to continue rubbing, stroking, fucking and I know if she doesn't stop he's going to — I'm going to come right here —

She stops suddenly, whirling him around so that I can see his cock outlined under the denim, his eyes closed and his hands reaching out for Nat's hips to pull her back to him. She gently pushes his hands away, and then takes him by the hand again and turns to leave the bar. As I follow them quietly, I notice that the woman who's checking IDs at the door has been watching us, and as I leave, she briefly touches my shoulder, not meeting my eyes.

On the street, I stay about forty feet behind the identical pair who are walking in step ahead of me, in the hazy streetlights. The sidewalks are that deep inside-eyelid red of cloudy nights and the air is still enough so that I can hear that the pair in front of me are not talking. When we finally walk up the sidewalk to our house, I hear Nat speak for the first time. She's telling him just to wait, not to touch her until she says it's okay. He nods and leans against the pillar of our porch with his hands in his pockets and his head back.

Nat finally gets the door open and holds it so that he can go in. She leaves it ajar, and I follow them a couple of minutes later.

When I get to our living room, I see that Nat has already lit candles and put on music — more Margo. The man has taken off his jacket and is sitting, waiting for instruction, taut. Nat is lighting candles, telling him the rules. "I'm going to fuck you. You know I'm going to fuck you. And it will be worth it. I'm going to let you slide that rock hard cock of yours into my wanting butch cunt, you'll like that won't you, you've never fucked a dyke quite like me before, have you? But you have to obey the rules. Will you do that?" She stops as she asks him the question. He nods, reaching for her. She laughs and pushes him away. "You haven't said it. Say it."

"Yes. Of course." He's still reaching for her, trying to get her to stop moving around, trying to bring her back to where she left him in the bar.

"You don't even know the rules yet." She laughs. "Rule number one is you don't touch me, you don't do anything, until I say you can. That includes coming. You don't come until I say you can. I mean that. You'll wear a condom. And when I'm ready, I'm going to fuck you in the ass."

He looks up, surprised, and she laughs again. "I'm a dyke — I have my own cock. And it's going to be in your ass, hard, fucking you, when I'm ready. The final rule is my lover gets to watch. You don't touch her, she doesn't touch you, and I don't touch her — but she gets to watch. She doesn't talk or participate — she just watches. And you can watch her." She finished preparing the room and hung up her jacket, pulling the bag with the sex toys and condoms and lube out of the closet.

"Turn around." She walks over to him and sits behind him as I make myself comfortable in my familiar chair in the corner, out of her way. She begins to massage his shoulders deftly, her fingers working into his muscles. As he relaxes, she eases him onto the wide couch and begins working down his back, pausing at his ass. She kneads his ass as he begins pressing his cock into the sofa, grinding and circling with his hips. He reaches around and tries to touch her tits, her arms, her shoulders, and she manoeuvres herself out of his reach, still kneading his ass, circling underneath on the tops of his thighs, and finally running her finger up the sensitive cleft. He continues to grind, and she reaches around, unbuttoning his Levi's and pulling them off. He lies there in his t-shirt and long Calvins, trying to turn around, but she keeps one strong hand on his back, holding him down. "You want it, don't you? You're thinking about my cunt and you haven't even seen it yet. You're not going to touch it yet — but you'll have your chance to touch it, to fuck it. It's wet for you — your hard cock makes me wet. But I'm not ready for you yet. First I'm going to sweetly stroke your asshole through your underwear like this."

As she talks, she continues to fuck the crack of his ass with her fingertips, pausing at his asshole to insert her finger gently. He begins to softly ask her to fuck him. Please. To touch him. Please. To let him fuck her. She continues to fuck him through his underwear, letting her fingers dance down to cup his balls and to stroke his cock. I watch as she reaches under to grab his cock, to stroke, to fuck it with her hand, and to deftly roll him around, never letting go of his cock, until he's lying on his back. She reaches under the couch and produces a set of velcro hand cuffs which she swiftly encases his wrists in, securing them to the end of the couch.

As I watch, my body grows calmer, moves into the plateau stage of arousal where I know there is no going back. The urgency is replaced with knowing, with a deep conviction of wet filling lust. I gently insert my hand into my pants and tease my clit, my other hand under my breast, gently cupping and stroking.

I slide my finger into my cunt, feeling the wash of wetness swell around me, stroking my clit, as I watch my powerful lover speak to this man, tease him into groaning, compliant desire. She continues to speak to him as she undoes her buttons, letting her white shirt fall open and expose her full brown wanting breasts, the lazy wide nipples taut with arousal. She unbuttons her own Levi's, easing them down over her strong legs. "Do you want me?" She leans over and pulls down his underwear, stroking his cock, his hard dick with the glistening drop on the end, stroking, pulling his cock into red swollen hardness. She leans over and gently licks his cock, letting her tongue roll over the wetness on the end, taking the end of his cock into her mouth, sucking hard, pulling, a purple flush as he begins to lift himself into her mouth. She laughs softly and lets go of him, murmuring, "You really want that, don't you? But I'm not going to do that..." She trails her fingertips down against his balls, her fingers kneading visibly under his underwear.

"Do you want to put it in me? If you ask nicely, I'll let you put it in me, but just for a second." She moves her body so that she's straddling him, the warmth of her wet cunt stretching around his hardness through their twin Calvins. He begins to thrust against her, talking. Talking. Please. Please let me, just for a second, I feel you wet, I want to fuck you, you'll like it...I promise you, I'll just put it in you for a minute, please, I want it. I want to put it in you. Feel that, feel my hardness — you won't be able to stop — can you feel yourself fucking against it — yes, fuck against it, just like that — please, I want it — yes, fuck me like that — oh, you want, I can feel your clit through your underwear — you want. Let me, please — oh — just for a minute, I promise, just for a minute, please — just let me put it in you — let me, please — I want to fuck it — yes pull down my underwear like that my god please yes undo me undo my cuffs please let me turn over like that —

"I'll undo you — but don't forget, you promised. I'm going to let you fuck me slowly. Oh please, yes, beg like that — you can't forget who's in charge here. I'm going to undo your hands, but I'm not going to take my underwear off, you have to fuck against me, on top of me, like that. Yes, up, god you're hard, god I want you inside me — feel my cunt, put your fingers there. Yes that's where I want it — good — just like that — yes yes I said 'turn over' yes like that over oh please."

She groans deep, guttural, inside herself as she pulls a latex glove over her hand and slides her finger covered in lube inside his ass fucking hard, feeling him.

She comes as I cling to her in our bed, my latex-clad hand unfurling hard and deep inside her, safe.

DEB ELLIS

Down on the Docks

One night in early autumn I was gripped by a too-familiar restlessness. I decided to try a new antidote, one that might take the edge off my need and allow me to remain in my humdrum life a little longer.

I took the streetcar as far as it would go and walked a good two miles after that, down to the docks. Not the tourist docks, with the gift shops and silly party boats; the real docks, where goods are exchanged, longshoremen sweat, and sailors haunt the landscape trying to recapture land legs and love. I had never been there before — fear keeping me from its shadows and unknown corners — but on this night, restlessness was stronger than fear.

The thin sound of a tinny juke-box drew me into a tavern in the basement of an old warehouse. I was greeted by clouds of cigarette smoke thicker than the fog outside. I stepped down the stairs into a dimly lit den of sailors and dock workers, most of whom were either passed out or were on the verge of doing so. I made my way over prostrate bodies to the bar, where the only alert patron was sitting. I slid onto a stool a few seats away from her. "Whisky — straight," I said to the barkeeper. I needed something to take the chill off my bones and the edge off my nerves.

I stole glances at my neighbour. Even through the loose folds of her white sailor suit I could sense the strength of the muscles in her arms. Her white sailor cap was parked at an angle at the back of her head. Her short, black curls spilled out around her face and neck.

She raised her head and caught me looking at her. She had the deepest eyes I had ever seen. Even in the murky tavern, they were magnets, pulling me in. For a long moment she just looked, then she smiled, a small, amused upturn of her mouth that said to me, "What took you so long?"

My whisky came. I gulped it down, acting cool and tough, but I started to choke. My cough corresponded with the end of the lousy torch song that had been playing on the juke-box. The sailor left her stool. I was afraid I'd blown it. She dug coins out of the pocket of her bell bottoms, fed them into the juke-box, and unhurriedly walked back towards me.

She didn't even ask me to dance. She just pulled me off the bar stool. By the time we got to the puny dance floor, the music had kicked in, a rich, bluesy song, sung by a woman with the world in her voice. The sailor pulled me close to her. I wonder how she knew that was what I was there for. Perhaps she didn't. Perhaps she was only answering her own need, quenching her own thirst.

The feel of her excited me. I allowed myself to indulge that excitement. I did not have to hold back, as I do in the dyke bars. I did not have to wonder who she'd slept with last, if she knew my old lovers, if my being with her like this was going to have repercussions in the community, or if she was going to try to make inroads into my life that I didn't want. She was a sailor, my sailor. All I needed to know about her was that she felt good in my arms.

The song ended. I moved to break away from her, unsure of what she wanted. She held on. There was no way she was going to let me go back to my bar stool. I looked into her face. I was sure she could sense me melting between my thighs.

The music started up again. She drew me close, more slowly this time, as if she knew I was hooked. My sailor was not shy with her hands. They began to roam over my body, underneath my jacket. My fingers began to dance in her hair, stroke the skin on the back of her neck where it met the wide collar of her uniform.

She stepped back a little, placed my arms at my sides, then reached up and slipped off my jacket. It slid to the floor. When her hands came up to me again, they brushed the sides of my breasts. It felt as though she had x-ray eyes, and could see through my green work shirt and jeans to my skin.

I bent my head, just slightly, and we kissed. Her lips were open and moved against mine in a perfect rhythm. My tongue caressed hers, touched it in little tips of touch as though it were too hot to commit to. Then I committed.

She shoved a muscled thigh between my legs and we leaned into each other. She danced us to the darkest corner of the dance floor, then reached for my shirt. Her fingers slipped into the space between the buttons and grazed my skin. I kissed her as she undid and opened my shirt. My breasts were there for the taking.

My sailor made me suffer. My nipples ached for her but she made them wait.

She knew her way around the tavern. Reaching behind

her, she opened a door, and pulled me through. We were on the docks. Without breaking stride, she led me to a large bundle of rags tied together, and backed me into it. The bundle was chest high, and as large as a bed. She pushed me firmly against it, took my arms in her hands and pinned them to the sides of the bundle.

She kissed me, hard, then moved to my throat. Her lips were powerful, her tongue thick and strong. She sucked at the nape of my neck then finally reached my breasts. She kept her leg pressed between my thighs as she circled my nipples with her wonderful tongue then clamped her mouth to them, with powerful suction. I couldn't move, and didn't want to.

She released my hands. I brought them immediately to her full, round breasts and kneaded them through her uniform. I started to remove her shirt, but she had other ideas.

Her hands were between my legs. She smiled at how soaked I was through my jeans. She pulled down my zipper, snapped open the clasp, then, bending down, lifted me on top of the bundle.

I tried to remain sitting but she pushed me onto my back and fixed my arms in place with the ropes which held the bundle together. She yanked my jeans down a bit. My underwear was in her way. I heard the sound of an opening jackknife then felt the cold steel against my hot flesh as it sliced through the thin material.

She spread me out. I felt her hot breath as it mixed with cool, damp fog. I could not see her. I could see nothing but dark mist occasionally slightly illuminated by the flashing red light of a far off lighthouse. She was going to take her time, and I was going to have to let her.

Her hands held my legs as far apart as my half down jeans would let my legs be spread. I could feel the strength of her fingers on the inside of my thighs. Her fingertips were rough and hard from hard work and salt water. She began nibbling around my cunt, keeping to the outer edges. I wanted to grab her head, force her mouth where I needed it most but I could not move my arms.

Suddenly she was there. The tip of her tongue touched the tip of my clit and stayed there. I was so turned on that even this slight tough started me coming. She pulled back. She blew on me to cool me down. Her fingers played rhythms along my thighs. She wanted to eat me, and she wanted me to control myself while she did it.

She parted my vaginal lips gently with her teeth, then began to lick me and work her tongue deep into my cunt. Each movement filled me with fire.

This was way beyond anything I had ever done before — being tied up while a woman I had never spoken to, whom I had just met, drove me crazy with her tongue.

When she knew I couldn't stand it any more, she brought her mouth up to my clit and started doing to it what she had done to my nipples. Suddenly she plunged her thumbs deep into me, one into my cunt, one into my ass, alternating rhythms so that one went in while the other moved out. I came then, in a shattering explosion of light and sensation.

I wanted her now but everything was still on her terms. She climbed up onto the bundle and shucked her uniform. She hovered over me so I could reach her cunt with my tongue. The fog settled in her pubic hair and created tiny drops of moisture in the dark curls. She tasted of the four winds and the seven seas. She tasted of women all over the world she had already had, and was to have before her travels were through.

She took her cunt from my mouth and replaced it with her breasts. Stretched out on top of me, she undid my bindings, then moved me higher on the bundle, so my legs no longer dangled. Reaching down, she yanked off my jeans, then started to fuck me rapidly with her fingers. She laughed at how hot I was.

When I was almost ready to come again, she moved between my legs to rub herself against me. Her cunt was as hot and as wet as my own. We came at the same instant.

My sailor collapsed on top of me. We stayed like that for awhile, then sat up and helped each other dress. She jumped down from the bundle first, then assisted me. She led me by the hand back into the tavern, helped me with my jacket, and grabbed her own peacoat from the back of a chair.

We held hands as we walked in silence down the road to where I had to turn off to go home. My sailor kissed me then and without a word, left me there. I stood for a moment, breathed in the fog, wondered if it had all been a dream. Then I turned around and saw, for the last time, my sailor walking slowly down on the docks.

April Miller

Butch Baiting

I love to make you sweat.

We don't see each other often but when we do I make sure I lay my hand on your arm, just so. My touch is soft and light. Just firm enough to feel your muscles clench. I watch your hands ball into fists.

Poor baby, you're fighting it.

I lean in close enough for you to catch my scent, feel my heat. I brush against you with my breasts, "accidentally" graze your back with my nipples. I like the way it feels. I like the feel of you. I like it when you flinch and start to tremble.

Poor butch. Poor big tough butch. I know you're getting wet, getting hard. Trapped between two femmes, between your girlfriend and the feel of my tits, you're trying to play it cool.

Cold. Hard. Stone. Butch.

"Dance with me." I watch the sweat break out on your

forehead. Watch you wait for your girlfriend's nod of permission.

Don't fool yourself, girl, she knows.

I grasp your hand. You respond to my pull, follow me to the dance floor. I know you are watching the sway of my hips. Feeling the tap of my heels on your clit.

We move into a field of gyrating bodies, the illusion of privacy. I slide my hands up your chest, over your shoulders. I drape my hands around the back of your neck. While I stare into your eyes as my fingertips glide through the buzz-cut hair at the nape of your neck, you finally reach out with your large capable hands and hold me. Press me to you, belly, breasts, thighs.

You're giving in.

I slide sideways a little and press my leg into your pussy, feel the damp heat of you there. Feel the stiffness and hunger of the erection you never wear in public. I stroke my fingers along the bulge on your thigh, cup you in my hand and listen to you gasp for breath. I feel your hips push insistently against mine.

I know what we want.

I watch your face as I toy with the buttons on your jeans. I kiss you once and when you push your tongue past my closed lips I grab hold, suck it deep into my mouth. I torment your tongue with my lips and teeth, work it like it's your cock I'm devouring.

When you break the kiss I unbutton your fly. Reach in and free your manhood, your hunger. I drop to my knees and rub your erection with my face, stroke it with my nose and hair. I take your balls behind my teeth. Suck them, twirl my tongue around them and let them go. Glide my tongue up and down the length of your shaft, around and over the tip. I flick my tongue lightly at the indentation until you press between my parted lips, through my mouth. Until you pound yourself deep into my throat.

I want you to grab my hair and fuck my face until you're screaming with pleasure. 'Til I am so hot and wet and open that when you slide out of my mouth and push me onto my back on the floor, you slowly pull up my miniskirt to my hips and discover my bare pussy framed by black garters and stockings, you spread my legs and settle your stocky, muscular body between them, and finally enter me with one hard practised thrust of your pelvis, I can take it.

I want to take you, take your cock and squeeze it with my pussy. Moan and sigh when you bite my neck and pinch my nipples. Gouge your back with my nails and beg you to fuck me until you lose all control and thrust us to an orgasm wherein we shatter into tiny pieces and lay trembling on the floor.

Until the song ends.

I unhook my fingers from your hair. You drop your gaze and step back to remove your thigh from my cunt, my cunt from your thigh. We pretend not to notice the girl-slime on your pants, your erect nipples, shortness of breath.

It's true, I dance sleazy with everyone.

As I watch you walk back and sit down next to your girlfriend, I know you're going to have sex with her tonight. She'll put on frilly underwear and spread her legs for her big "man."

Inside, you'll be calling my name.

JOAN NESTLE

Woman of Muscle, Woman of Bone

Dedicated to jock butches, a wonder of their own.

Her body covered me with a cape of muscled strength. Her voice, that controlled trained voice, found another register, and she said my name in long expulsions of breath. With each emptying of her lungs, she lunged her knee between my legs, pushing my large full thighs further apart. I was on my stomach under her, my head turned on the pillow, my sweat marking the tension of being so completely held. Each time she pulled herself up for another thrust, I could see her. Just the tip of her. Her short grey hair, her neck swollen with her exertions but made delicate by the beaded necklace that hung just away from the thickened muscle. Then the push would come, and I could see nothing. My whole body absorbed the impact through my cunt that was so wet it dripped upon the sheets, up into my stomach and into my breasts which shook and grew larger under the impact. My whole body absorbed that one move and braced for the next.

My arms were stretched out on either side of me, her hands gripped my own. In the pauses between her mountings, I pressed my lips against the hardness of her forearms, against the cords of muscle. I tried to bite into her flesh but there was no skin that hung freely. All was stretched to its limit to cover the swell of muscle. Like the corded ropes of a ship's railing, her arms kept me from falling and I turned my cheek into her hardness, caressing the safety of her muscles.

She had worked very hard for each ridge, each swell of sculptured flesh. Sometimes while I lay in bed waiting for her, I imagine her in the gym where she had chosen to wage the battle against smallness. I can see her in her grey sweatpants and white t-shirt, sitting on a bench, her legs spread wide into a V, her back arched, her body tilted over her working arm and her left hand braced on her inner thigh. She curls her arm over and over, the weights like Sisyphean stones she cannot let go. Her head is turned in a concentrated stare as if to will the muscle into new growth. Her repeated movements, a chant against the body's frailty.

After innumerable curls, she moves on to her next and next task, always weighing her body down, so resistance itself becomes both a comrade and an enemy. Here in this mirrored place, women's bodies bend in a devoted dance, pushing and pulling their flesh into newly muscled forms.

Finally, I come to her when she is drenched in sweat and finished with the endless battle for this day. I come to her and stand before her, my body soft, full and marked with aging. I push her back against the wall. She falls into it as if its hardness is a pillow. I run my hands over her trembling muscles, over her almost breastless chest where flesh has fled. I find her nipples, the pouting remnants and I tease them over and over again, forcing her to feel another kind of muscle tightness.

When her nipples are hard knots, I reach up and force her head down so she has to see my red nails flagrantly decorative, outlining her ridges. I deepen their touch so her muscle is indented by femme persistence. My hands move over her belly, now transformed into a thick egg resting in a nest of bone. I stay on her belly for a long time, pushing, caressing, circling its firmness until she moves forward from the wall, pushing her hips towards me. So much yearning in the bone.

I push her back, letting her know I will not accept her impatience. Soon her breath quickens and a new sheen of sweat shines upon her skin. I lean forward and lick drops of her body's wetness off her chest, lingering in the hollow of her throat. Now she knows what I will do and all her strength cannot stop me. I stand straight in front of her, close but not resting on her. She senses my certainty, smells my perfume and tenses.

"You know what I am going to do."

Her head turns, following the words. Her eyes are still closed.

"Oh Joan, oh God," she implores. My hand moves down to her hips, to her lower belly, to her thighs. I peel off her pants as I travel, letting them fall to her ankles. She stands naked before me. Her body is arched, hungry, tight. I enjoy all that I see with a deep appreciation for her work and with a delight at what I can bring her. I move closer, my breath touching her. After a silence, a protracted moment of suspended action, I cup her cunt in my hand. Her wetness is already seeping through. My red nails are petals of crimson against her wiry hair. Now she rests in my palm, her small-est muscle is throbbing in my hand. My body moves behind each rubbing, pushing her harder against the wall, pushing her into her own rhythm of want. Suddenly, knowing she is ready, I seize her turned head and with a quick move, enter her, reminding her of the waiting, wanting, softness beneath the bone.

This was my dream as I lay in the bed waiting for her, my fantasy of gratitude and appreciation. She appears wear-ing her white cotton gi, her body oiled and laced with beads of water. Like two ancient wrestlers, we assume our posi-tions. I on my stomach and she lowered upon me. The weight of her is pushing the dream from my mind but I remember the power of my taking and I feel a surge of my own resistance — my refusal to be just a body under her that takes her strength without a voice of its own.

Throughout the days of life, I too have built muscle. My body tightens under her. I harden the center of my back and push up against her, carrying her whole long body with me, announcing my refusal to be intimidated by her strength. Her delight at my resistance, expressed in low laughter that turns to moans, gives me the victory I want. She hangs against my ass, pushing herself into it, trying to get more and more of it against herself. For a moment, I hold both of us, our weights now joined. I balance on my elbows. My head bends low between my breasts, which have fallen out of my nightgown. I am now my own kind of athlete. She is marooned above the bed, lifted high on my back, curled over my fullness.

She pushes, rocks, groans and then there is silence. I know what is coming. I can almost hear her body laughing as she reaches under me. If she is kind, she pushes out one elbow and then the other until I fall with a rush, flat on my stomach. When she is more impatient, she simply takes me down and places her hand between my shoulder blades, like an anchor, while with the other, she reaches inside of me, bringing me home on waves of strong steady movement.

Woman of muscle, woman of bone, I have not known your kind before.

Karen X. Tulchinsky

The Gay Divorcée

Five months ago, my whole life changed.

One week before our sixth anniversary Jacquie dumped me for Spike Goldstein, a softball player and accountant who lives in our apartment building, two floors down. I almost fell over in shock. I hadn't seen it coming. We were sitting at the kitchen table eating supper and as the reality of what she said settled in, my fajita-filled fork clattered onto my plate and my heart exploded in my chest. Her words were a blur, as if I was listening to someone speak a foreign language. I heard only fragments of her sentences, isolated words and half-thoughts.

"Can't go on like this...over...still be friends...haven't been happy...you know as well as I do...we've been moving apart...sorry...hurts me too..." She cried while she spoke.

I sat in my seat, mouth gaping, and stared. My pulse raced adrenalin through my veins. Her decision shot through me, splintering my heart into a million tiny pieces, ripped a hole in my chest clear through to the other side.

Strangely, I was also calm, resigned. Loss was nothing new to me. My friend Alex died of AIDS five years ago, my grandfather passed away shortly after and I lost my friend Judy to AIDS last September. The knowledge that Jacquie was not dying, only leaving, was the one thought that held me together. I sat, listened and did not speak. What was there to say?

For months I wallowed in despair, shock, pain and humiliation. Jacquie and I had been known in the community as one of the few long term couples who were "making it." Although we hadn't wanted it, we were role models for other women. During the first three months of our breakup I was so raw and exposed I could barely leave the house. Every cell in my body vibrated with pain. I'd go to sleep sad and wake up horrified. My pride, self-esteem and ego plummeted to new depths, tossed off a twenty-story building to splatter on a grease-covered back alley, all alone and badly bruised. While Jacquie and Spike lived happily ever after, I drank too much scotch, showed up late for work, watched "I Love Lucy" reruns, cried on friends' shoulders, smoked grass, felt sorry for myself, made rude comments in public about my ex and her current, cried, carried on and gradually became known throughout town as a bitter homosexual.

Bitter or not, I have never been the celibate type. I like sex too much for that. I knew I could be in misery and grief and fucking my brains out at the same time. And I was out to prove it. There was no doubt about my pain. You could see it on my face, feel it exude from my body, hear it echo through my broken heart and thrash around inside my empty belly. I knew that in the end, only time would heal me. Deep in fog I sensed I had to rebuild my broken pride from within, nurse my own wounds until I could reaffirm my reason to live. Find strength in my own heart and learn how to love myself. In the loneliest, bleakest hours of our lives, our selves are all we can really count on. But, for the moment my thinking was far more shallow than that. I needed to be appreciated. I wanted to be chased. I wanted to be loved, held, stroked, licked, kissed, touched and taken. My body cried out for caresses, and, even in my sorrow, I was horny as hell. After five months of suffering, I was moving to a new emotional place.

"If you know anyone who's ever had a crush on me," I told all my friends, "give her my phone number and tell her it's a good time to call."

My mission had begun. Or so I thought. After six years of marriage to Jacquie, I was out of practise. A lot of things had changed in that time. Women were younger. There was safe sex to worry about. I had aged. I wasn't sure if women would still find me attractive. I wasn't sure where to start. I was beside myself with panic. I ran to the phone and called Bobby Silverstein, my cousin and big time babe-ifyer about town.

"Okay," she said. "We'll start with the obvious. Who do you have the hots for?"

I thought about it and drew a blank. "I don't know."

"What?"

"I haven't been looking, Bobby. You know that."

"Kayla. You can't think of anybody? Someone you know from the gym? The bar? How about work?"

No one came to mind.

"Come on. There must be somebody."

"I told you. I haven't been looking."

"Well, looking is the first thing you have to be doing. Are you sure there isn't somebody?"

"Of course I'm sure. I was happily married."

"Kayla, it's me you're talking to. I know you've looked

around. You've told me yourself. Wasn't there some woman you were lusting after just last year?"

"No! I already told you. I can't think of anyone. Okay?"

"Oh boy."

"What?"

"This might be harder than I thought."

"Don't say that," I groaned. "You're depressing me."

"Okay. Sorry. Look, I'll be right over. We can't do this over the phone. You're in bad shape."

"Oh, thanks."

"Go take a shower or something to clear your head. I'll be there in half an hour."

She brought over a six pack of beer, warm, but we opened two anyway and a copy of *Flaunt It*, our local queer paper. Bobby spread it open on my coffee table at the classified ads section. Bright red marker already circled a few ads. Bobby dialled the phone number and thrust the receiver into my hand. A computer voice explained the rules.

"Welcome to Queer Connections classified ads. A charge of ninety-six cents a minute will automatically be billed to your home number. At the tone, punch in the box number of an ad that interests you."

I chose one of the circled ads. A woman's voice repeated the printed ad word for word, then asked me to leave a message after the tone. I eyed Bobby for help. She shrugged.

"Uh...," I began eloquently, "I saw your ad." Oh brilliant. "And, uh, I live in Vancouver and I'm recently single and...," I referred to the ad, "I see that you like to go dancing. So, uh, let's meet. Okay? I...look forward to meeting — uh, hearing from you. Okay. Bye." I banged down the receiver.

Bobby shook her head. "You forgot to leave your phone number."

"Oh shit. You think I should call her back?"

"I don't know. She'll either think it's endearing or she'll think you're a nerd. Hard to say."

"Oh great. I'm not calling back. This is nerve-wracking."

"Uh huh." Bobby re-dialled the number and handed me the receiver.

"Again?"

"Pick a different box number."

I tried another one. A soft and sexy voice said she was a well-endowed femme looking for butches to satisfy her. No walks on the beach, movies or dinners, she just wanted sex. I left my first name, my number and tried to sound sexy, charming, witty and intelligent. I hung up the phone and beamed.

Bobby picked it back up. "Do more. They won't all call back."

"Really?"

"Uh huh."

I called all the ads Bobby had circled.

"Now what?"

"Well, it'll take a few days before you get any responses, so now we go to the bar."

"What? Bobby, I've barely even looked at another woman in six years. Don't you think this is enough for one night?"

"Hell no. Come on. You've been miserable and depressed for six months."

"Five," I broke in defensively.

"Okay five. Enough is enough. It's time to get out there. So go put some gel in your hair. We're going out."

I sighed and trundled somewhat reluctantly into the bathroom.

At the club I bought us each a beer. We stood near the dance floor, watching. The bar was in a basement, with low ceilings and black walls. The carpet was red. Purple black-lights lit up every piece of fluff on dark shirts, white tee-shirts glowed fluorescent and everyone's teeth looked green. In the centre of the dance floor, a medium-sized disco ball bounced small beams of white light all around the room, circling and spinning.

Bobby was telling me a tasteless joke about blonde travel agents when I saw Ana. I couldn't remember her name at first, but I remembered her. Long black curly hair, deep dark eyes, a full mouth, cheekbones for days and a curvy volup-tuous body encased in tight black spandex shorts poking out under a short purple skirt. On top she wore nothing but a black sports bra. She had the widest smile and the warmest eyes. From across the room, I was instantly enchanted, as I had been once before. We had met over a year ago. We'd talked and I'd bought her a drink. We'd danced, laughed. Then I walked her to her car, where we kissed. Melted into each other, without a word, riding with the night air, the wind. Until I remembered I was married. Remembered who I was and the choices I had made. I broke from her grasp suddenly. Without explanation, I ran. And did not look back.

Now, here she was again, on the other side of the bar dancing with someone I'd never seen before. I watched, trying to determine if they were friends or lovers. They danced a few feet apart, occasionally leaning in toward each other to talk and laugh. When they danced, they looked around more than they looked at each other. Definitely friends, I decided. No sexual heat between them. I looked over, Bobby was staring at me.

"Who are you looking at?" She strained above the music.

I nodded my head toward the dance floor. "That's Ana."

"Who?"

"Remember? I met her last year. She used to live here. She's from Mexico City. I almost went home with her one night, that time when Jacquie was back east visiting her family. Remember?"

Bobby pointed her finger at me. "I told you! I knew there was someone."

I shrugged sheepishly. "Nothing much happened. I walked her to her car and we kissed. Then I chickened out and bolted." I shook my head. "She probably thought I was a total nerd. Last I heard she was living in California. Haven't seen her since."

Bobby looked over at Ana, checking her out. "So that's her? Looks good."

"Good? Are you crazy? She's beautiful."

"So? If that's how you feel, go ask her to dance."

"You think I should?"

Bobby shook her head and frowned at me.

"Okay. I'm going."

As I crossed the dance floor to Ana, I recalled when I'd kissed her by her car. I'd spoken to her in Spanish. I didn't know much, but I did know how to say, *Que bonitos ojos tienes*, What beautiful eyes you have, and when I told her, she smiled back at me and moved closer. It was one of those perfect moments. The night was warm. Music drifted across the street from the club. Her perfume lured me closer. Her brown eyes drew me in. My lips were on hers. My arms were around her waist. Her soft body pressed against me. I was floating away on a wave of desire, cheating on my girlfriend and I couldn't stop myself. Her mouth felt too good on mine, her kisses too sweet, her touch too tantalizing, our passion too potent. We wrapped our arms around each other until we were crazy with hunger. She asked me to come home with her. I wanted to, but the consequences of crossing that line were more than I was prepared to deal with. I ran. It was the last time I saw her.

I crossed the dance floor and stopped a few feet from Ana. She looked at me blankly. Then her face lit up, "Hola," her beautiful brown eyes smiled.

"Como estas?" I grinned back.

"Bien, gracias. I'm back in Vancouver."

"I can see that."

"Momentito." She held up a finger and leaned over, whispering something to her friend. Her friend looked over at me and shrugged, then walked off the dance floor.

"Dance?" Ana asked.

"It would be my pleasure."

I started to move my hips and arms to the music, careful to keep a few feet back, to give her space. She moved right up against me, pushing her pelvis seductively in my direction. My heart fluttered and I felt my whole body respond. I swallowed hard and smiled at her.

She came in real close and whispered in my ear, "So? How are things with you?"

"Okay. Me and Jacquie broke up."

She backed away and looked me in the eye. "Oh." She shook her head, then moved back in. "How are you doing?"

"Okay. It's been hard. I'm much better now." I slipped an arm around her waist. She rested a hand on my shoulder and we danced through the rest of the song. She had a sexy femme way of dancing, moving her hips in a circular motion, lightly touching my thighs with all parts of her body. With her free hand, she held the edge of her skirt and swung it around. Tight spandex shorts covered her skin like black paint. She kept her face close to mine. I could almost feel her lips on my skin. I wanted to kiss her. We danced on through the next three songs.

"You know, I think about you sometimes," she whispered.

"You do?"

"Uh huh." She grazed her lips against my neck. "I wonder what might have happened between us, if we had continued that night." Her tongue darted inside my ear. Oh my God. This was too good to be true. My first night out as a single babe and I had a beautiful woman wrapped in my arms, talking sweet, looking sexy. A miracle. She was flirting with me. No, more than that. She was cruising me. My stomach turned over. I wasn't sure what to do next.

She pulled back again and gazed at me. I stared into her serious eyes. She inched toward me. Her lips were calling out. There was only one thing to do. I leaned forward and kissed her, lightly. She threw her arms around my neck and kissed me hard. I squeezed her to me, kissing her, long and deep, tongue around tongue. The taste of her was inside me, rushing down to my liquid belly, circling, rising with the rhythm of her breath. My senses heightened, intensified with memories of the time we kissed before. I opened my eyes to look at her. She was beautiful. I kissed her face, her long eyelashes. She moaned. I moved down to her neck, tasted the salt of her sweat. She was pressing her cunt against my leg. My blood pulsated, pounded in my belly, stirring delicious pleasure, rising in sweet, slow, searing waves.

"Hey. Why don't you two get a room?" a voice asked. We stopped kissing and glanced over. A woman dancing beside us smirked.

"Isn't this a room?" I shot back, pleased with myself for being so witty.

Ana laughed, and then gave me a solemn, sexy look. She grasped my hand, squeezed it and put it around her waist. "Maybe she's right," she said.

"Mmmm," I agreed, smiling at her.

"How about my place?"

"Are you inviting me?"

"You know I am."

"Hang on a second." I went over to tell Bobby I was leaving.

"You rogue," she winked at me. "I want all the details tomorrow."

"Thanks for dragging me out." I raced back to Ana.

At her car, she opened the doors and we slipped in. Ana was behind the wheel. She turned to me. I slid sideways, close to her. She grabbed the collar of my jacket, pulling me to her. We kissed in a fury. Wild, intense, urgent and passionate. We moaned. I reached up and caressed one of her breasts with my hand.

"Oh god," she said. "Come on. Let's go to my place."

"Okay." Still leaning over her, I kissed her neck and squeezed her nipple between my fingers.

"Okay." She pressed against my hand, making no move to start the car.

"Good idea." I leaned into her lips and we kissed again. Sweet pains in my belly dripped down my body to my cunt.

"Okay," she repeated, breathless.

"Okay," I whispered back, running my tongue along her neckline.

"Oohh." Her hands strayed around to the back of my neck and into my hair.

"You smell great." My tongue explored the space between her breasts.

"You feel amazing," she reclined further back against the door frame.

We couldn't get enough. We were left-brain lesbians, focused on nothing but our bodies, hurtling through white water rapids, spinning and swirling, down a rushing river, our passion unrestrained.

"Okay." She tore herself away, pushed me back to the passenger seat. I was breathing hard. We both were. I bent to kiss her again.

"Stop," she laughed. "We'll never get home this way."

Ana started the car and pulled out into traffic. I clasped her free hand and held it as we drove. We felt up each other's hand, squeezing and stroking, grabbing and holding. I brought hers to my lips, sucking and biting her middle finger. She turned to me, her eyes smouldering. I rubbed her whole hand all over my face. She broke free, ran her fingers through my curly black hair.

"Where do you live?" I asked breathless.

"Not far." She panted. "Just off Commercial Drive."

"Me too."

I brought her roaming hand down to my lap, left it on my thigh as my fingers travelled slowly up her bare arm. I could feel goose bumps form on her skin. I caressed her harder, up to her shoulder and back down again. I leaned closer and kissed her neck. I felt the car make a sharp right turn and then it stopped. She threw the gear stick into park and reached for me, hands on both sides of my face. We kissed furiously, grunting and moaning, tongues and teeth, exploring and sucking. I didn't know if we were in her driveway or somebody else's. I didn't care. I pushed her back against the car door. The plastic panel between the bucket seats dug painfully into my side, as I struggled to get as close to her as I could. She grabbed at my t-shirt, trying to get it over my head. We knocked something down. She gave up on my shirt and plunged her hands underneath it, groping for my tits. I kissed up and down her neck. My legs were squeezed together tight and my hot clit throbbed. Her skirt was hiked up and she opened her legs wider. I thrust my pelvis into her crotch. I tugged at the waistband of her shorts.

"Querida," she kissed my lips, her tongue a torrential downpour of pent-up lust. I tumbled alongside her, carried away in a flood of fervent desire. "Let's go inside." Her hands gripped my shoulders. "It's too small in here."

Inside, she led me right to her bedroom. The blinds were open and moonlight fell across the bed. I waited in the middle of the room as she lit a candle and placed a CD into a portable player on her dresser. She sauntered toward me and threw her arms around my neck. I held her waist. She started to dance with me.

"Pretend we are still in the bar," she whispered in my ear, urgently. "We are on the dance floor, like before." She pressed her body up against mine, raised her face up to me and we kissed. We were breathing faster as I reached over and removed her bra. Her nipples were erect.

"Squeeze them," she said. "I like it hard. Yeah. That's good."

She tore at my t-shirt, peeled it off and tossed it on the floor.

"We are still in the bar," she said, rubbing against my naked chest, "and I want you to fuck me." She seized three fingers on my right hand and squeezed them. I moaned again. I eased her shorts and skirt down to her ankles. She stepped out of them and slid her naked body up and down my legs. I groped into my back pocket for a small leather case, which I opened. I removed a latex glove and grazed it all over her skin. I dropped to my knees and licked her leg, from the ankle up. I rubbed my shoulder against her clit as I rose to my feet again.

"I want you inside me," she insisted.

I snapped the glove onto my hand, kissed her, furiously and reached down. Even through the gloves I could feel how wet she was. Slippery. Warm. Her need engulfed the tips of my fingers. I slid one in.

"Oh god," she said. "We are still in the bar. Everyone is watching. You are fucking me in the bar."

Her fantasy burned through me. There was something torridly sexy about taking her on the dance floor in front of other hot babes. "Oh yeah, you're so wet. So open. Ready for me."

"Yeah, baby. More. Put more in."

I did as she asked. She took three of my fingers.

"Oh yeah," she said, "Just like that, slow. Uh huh. Oh yeah. Kayla. Fuck me."

"I am."

"Please."

"Yeah, baby."

"Don't stop."

"Never."

"Use your thumb on my clit," she ordered and gripped my hand to show me, as her tongue plunged inside my ear. "Slow circles. Okay?"

"Anything." My three fingers inside her, rotating slightly, my thumb worked circles around her hard, wet clit.

"Oh, baby." She was rocking on my fingers. "And now the bartender is walking over this way."

"Yeah?" I kept moving in circles, just how she liked it.

"She's mad at us."

"Uh huh?"

"She's going to kick us out. She's telling us to leave."

She moved faster on my thumb. Her breathing sped up. "But we can't stop. Oh, don't stop!" she screamed. "Please. Oh, please. Yeah. Oh, I'm going to come."

I was going to come too, just from listening to her. I kept rolling my thumb. I could feel her clit throb. I could feel her heart and pulse speed up. Her teeth clamped down on the skin on my neck. Pain and pleasure mixed and coursed through my blood.

"Yeah, Kayla. Oohh, baby, that's good. Ohhh, yeah!" She flung her whole body even tighter against me, impatiently lunged deeper onto my fingers. I sensed her spirit break free as her body convulsed on my hand. Her voice burst through the night air, loud and impetuous. Every part of her pulsed and quivered, aftershocks relentlessly trembled for a few minutes longer, as she came, again and again.

After a while her body relaxed. She slumped against my chest. I held her tightly around the waist and eased her over to the bed. We lay down and I held her in my arms. Her breathing calmed. Then it was kind of weird, because laying in Ana's arms like that, I thought about Jacquie. In my sadness, I hugged Ana tighter. Her body felt nice, warm and soft, womanly, but laying with her like that, made me think about my ex, my old life and everything I had lost. My eyes filled with tears, slowly rolling down my cheeks. Ana opened her eyes and wiped my face with her hand.

"It's okay," she murmured. But it wasn't. Nothing had been okay for a long time. I was at a change-point in my life and it was terrifying and lonely. I was on a journey, part way across a rickety, wooden, suspension bridge, high above a deep, mountain canyon. No railings or hand-guard, no safety net at all. And only room enough for one to pass. Far in the distance, the other side was barely visible, engulfed in a haze. It had no form, no shape. I couldn't see much of anything and I knew I wouldn't be able to for a long, long time. The unknowable future was frightening and I was afraid of every step toward it.

Six months ago I would have told you that Jacquie and I would be together forever. Who knows? Maybe we were. Maybe forever was just a little shorter than we originally thought.

STEPHANIE ROSENBAUM

Where You Want to Be

You are sitting at the bar mashing the chunk of lime in your gimlet, stabbing it over and over with the pointed end of a purple swizzle stick until the translucent, pulpy filaments splay out like an exhausted jellyfish. When the glass is empty, you'll spear the wan piece of lime and eat it whole, enjoying the bitter, vodka-edged tang of the dark green peel. But for now, you concentrate on the door. You are waiting for her.

Every week, on Wednesdays, you run the Pussycat Lounge, a retro-styled happy hour cabaret with Peggy Lee in the background and plates of diminutive pink and green canapés on each candlelit table. Your roommates are used to seeing you standing in the kitchen in seamed stockings and a beehive wig, hacking off the crusts of dozens of pimento cheese and cucumber sandwiches with a butcher knife. Your last girlfriend was an Elvis impersonator well versed in prom night fantasies, so you didn't need much time at the thrift store when this hostess job came up. There are white shirts and flannel pyjamas in your bureau drawers, but your closet is full of rustling navy taffeta, slinky cherry red satin and soft green lace lined in peach silk. Tonight you're wearing a full-skirted sleeveless summer dress of black pique. Flat black buttons run down the length of your dress, fastening it from the base of your neck to below your knees. You think of it as your Hedda Gabler-goes-to-Italy dress, stylish and severe, with only a wide black patent leather belt for ornamentation.

Underneath, you wear only sheer black stockings hitched up by a garter belt of dark red lace. It's too hot for a bra. Your breasts rub against the stiff ridges of the fabric as you go to tell the DJ to turn down the volume. It's early, not enough bodies yet to soak up the noise. But DJs are temperamental, and since this one has the best collection of lounge music you've ever seen, you bring a beer with your request. Plus, you're counting on her to play a couple of special requests tonight, so you want to keep on her good side. She takes the beer, rolls her eyes as you implore her not to turn the music up again. You have this exchange at least three times a night, every week.

A couple of women walk in, hesitating on the threshold. The Lounge occupies a space used as a punk club the rest of the week, and even candlelight and Nina Simone can't conceal the black walls and thrash-and-burn decor. You go into your hostess patter, easing them over to a table, taking their orders for a bourbon and soda and a lemon Calistoga. You chat them up until they relax and resume the conversation they'd begun outside. Discretely, you slip away, back to the mirror behind the bottles, where you can dab a fresh layer of Tres Tres Dior onto your lips and smooth a wet finger over the dark arches of your eyebrows. Where is she? It's nearly seven. She doesn't always come, but she knows this is where she can find you, all dressed up and waiting for her. Sometimes she dresses up too, not like the butch dandies strutting in their suits and ties, but like a sexy cowboy who doesn't need a big belt buckle or lizard boots to show off what she's got. You've always had a thing for Western girls, and this one can roll a cigarette with one hand while the other rests loosely on the steering wheel of her red pick-up truck, kiss and drive fast and eat biscuits sopped in gravy. She has a twang that she tries to hide and wears an arrowhead on a leather thong around her neck.

It's quarter to eight. The sweet fizz of anticipation in your stomach is beginning to flatten. It doesn't help that everyone asks where she is. You turn resolutely from the door and bite hard on the wedge of lime you've fished out of your empty glass. You want to be surprised, to feel her seeking you out. You suddenly get very busy making the rounds, bringing drinks, kissing cheeks, keeping the cocktail chat going. If she comes she'll find you busy. Maybe you'll make time for her. Then, a hand on your shoulder, a hand on your waist. You take off your glasses and lay them on the bar, leaning back into her lean hardness, her desert sage scent. She is a cowboy for you tonight. Her spurred boots are soft black leather, her black silk shirt is opened to show the flat planes of her collarbones. A Cherokee bracelet of turquoise bear claws and silver leaves wraps around one wrist. Her eyes are shadowed under a flat black hat gleaming with silver conchas.

The DJ has seen her. India Adams comes through the speakers, her voice a smoky purr, singing "Tame me, I'm a little wild, why don't you tame me? I'll be sweet and mild if you tame me..." You head onto the darkened dance floor, her hand holding your waist, pulling you closer until your bodies are pressed together from knees to shoulder. There is no mistaking the bulge between her legs, against her thigh.

The insistence of it is what you feel the most. The urgent, unassailable proof of desire that you remember from being with boys. It doesn't matter that this desire is inanimate, embodied in silicon rather than flesh. The very fact that she put it on before coming to see you, that she must have worn it all the way over here, feeling its weight riding between her legs, walking like a man down 16th Street, is proof enough. Her eyes are wicked. She knows you know. Her hand slides down to your ass, pulling you in so you are riding against it. She's bold tonight. You take a breath into the warm curve of her neck, run your tongue lightly up the curve behind her ear. You feel like Mae West in a roomful of sailors.

Other couples are coming onto the dance floor but you let her half dance, half walk you back to an alcove behind a stack of speakers. She looks at you expectantly, half grinning, half shy and you can't resist. Giggling, you breathe in her ear, "Is that a pistol in your pocket...or are you just happy to see me?" as you hitch yourself up onto the edge of a speaker, wrapping your legs around her waist. In answer, she runs a hand up the inside of your right leg, sliding your legs apart, lingering at the top of your stocking, running her fingers over the line where the sheer nylon stops and your flesh begins. Her mouth comes down over yours meeting your tongue in a shower of sparks. You catch her lower lip between your teeth as her hand reaches between your thighs to where your panties should be. "Tame me," you whisper as the red lights pulse over the couples swaying just inches away from where you are sitting, her hand under your skirt, shameless. Over the speakers even Petula

Clark is letting go, her chiming voice gone throaty and rich as she sings, "I don't want nobody else, cause I'm in love."

"What does it feel like, packing it?" you ask.

"Sexy," she replies, instantly. "And ready, like I could fuck you right here. Powerful," she adds as your nails travel down her back, tracing the furrows on either side of her spine. "Come home with me," she says and at the tone of her voice your heart quivers. The muscles in your stomach contract. With another stroke you could probably come right there behind the speakers but she takes her hand away and lifts you down onto the dance floor, leading you through the dancing couples and straight out the front door as you grab your leopard coat off the bar stool, your gimlet glass still standing empty above it.

She doesn't talk as she drives through the streets. You can barely breathe as she unlocks her front door. The hallway sparkles dimly from a string of white Christmas lights tacked waist-high along the wall. She hesitates on the threshold of her bedroom, then pulls open the door. Inside, the room is golden, glowing from candles flickering on the mantelpiece, in between the shells and bones of the fireplace altar and along the edge of the unfinished loft. The air is warm and close with the scent of sage and tobacco and hot candle wax. She presses you up against the door, kissing you as you let your coat slide down around your ankles. Your fingers are pulling her silk shirt out of her jeans, your cold hands running up her smooth stomach to cup her breasts, feeling her nipples harden with the chill of your fingertips. You twine your legs around her and the hardness is still there at the side of her thigh. She lifts her mouth from yours and asks, "Is this okay? Do you want to?" and you both know she's not just referring to the sex that is about to happen, that is already happening, but to the inclusion of this new thing, something she knows you've wanted but never done, something she's never done with a lover, not really, not like this. She's never had a woman want it like this from her, and you've never had a woman offer it, make herself strong, vulnerable and tough, her sexuality on raw display. You told a friend once, "I don't want a butch bottom, I want a butch top who'll give it up for me," and you whisper, "Yes, yes, I do, yes," feeling like Molly Bloom, just for an instant.

Her eyes are closed, their salt-green depths hidden in the shadow of her dark eyelashes. You are so close to her you can feel her ribs lifting as she takes a long slow breath, then exhales. "Suck my cock," she says, savouring the words, as though she's been waiting a long time to say that to somebody.

You remember the tricks your first boyfriend taught you. How to keep your lips over your teeth, work the sensitive spot just under the head with the tip of your tongue, take the whole length down your throat without gagging. You are down on your knees in front of her, reaching up to the buckle on her black leather belt. You think of the stories she tells about the guys who, thinking she's one of them, cruise her late at night as she backs her truck through the alley behind her apartment. About the men who lean against the walls, one hand hooked over the belt, the thumb of the other thrust deep in a rivet-edged pocket, fingers cupping the curve of the hard-on outlined against the thigh...but you don't have time for all this build up. This is too good. She's waited long enough.

You are pulling the wide strap of leather from behind the square silver buckle, unzipping her jeans, freeing her cock. You lick the tip, slowly teasing the head in and out of your mouth, running your hand up and down its firm, slightly spongy length as your thumb rubs against the swollen vein from base to tip. Her hand rests lightly on the top of your head as she leans back against the door, her legs loosely spread. Her fingers grip your hair, just barely at first, then tighter and tighter as you open your throat, feeling the hard length of it slide down, filling your throat as she rocks her hips against you, pushing and pulling the cock against the greedy suction of your open mouth. But you don't need her hands to guide you. The sounds coming from the back of her throat are enough to keep your mouth and tongue working their way up and down. You know that every stroke is pushing the base of the dildo against her swelling clit. Reaching up to stroke the balls wedged under the strap of the harness, you can feel the slippery wetness already soaking the black leather between her legs.

She doesn't want to come like this, not yet. Her fingers loosen their grip as she eases your head back, letting her dick slide out of your mouth to hang there, slick and ready. Out of her back pocket comes a flat square plastic package. You remember the orange and turquoise boxes that accompanied all your sex in college, the moments of rip-pause-snap during which you lay back, your eyes half-closed out of some unspoken respect for the privacy of the ritual. But there is no sound this time. The rubbery circle hasn't yet been sprung from its sealed envelope. Leaving it cupped in one palm, she leans down and takes your jaw between thumb and forefinger, gently, tilting your face up like something fragile and infinitely precious. The touch of her mouth on yours is soft, warm, cutting through your chest like a naked wire plunged into a torrent of icy water. Your heart contracts. You want to devour her, pull her soul into your mouth, sweep your tongue into every crevice of her, breathe her in like a drowning man gulping seawater. She is pushing you onto your back, pulling up your dress. "Spread your legs," she whispers, but you keep your slippery thighs pressed together. How much does she want it? Neither of you trust what comes too easily. You've only known each other a few weeks, but the tangles of desire and submission are pulling tighter and tighter with every urgent meeting, humming with tension like an electric wire singing high between the poles.

She stands over you, pulling her legs out of her jeans and boots until she is naked with the harness. Dark hair falls over her forehead, the arrowhead gleaming against her cinnamon skin. You reach up to slide each button out of its buttonhole, slowly laying yourself bare until you match her, skin for skin. Her green eyes run down your body. Hungry. Dazzled. You can deny her nothing. When she asks you again, her hand sliding between your clasped knees, you open your legs, slowly.

You are on your back, legs spread, knees bent. You take a sudden breath as she slides in, at the instant physical memory of penetration. You remember the first time you slept with a woman, after years of longing and how the real surprise was not her soft mouth or softer skin but the numerous ways in which it was utterly the same. Sex, skin, sensation, sweat. Even knowing she can't feel the dildo inside the hot velvety wetness of your cunt as your hips arch up to meet her, still you are connected to her like nothing else. Neither of you is pretending it's real. You want to be with a butch woman, not a man, and she knows that strapping it on doesn't make her male. But the silicon takes the heat of your body as she catches your rhythm and builds on it, dragging it out slowly so you can feel the friction of it. She holds it there just at the entrance to your cunt, teasing until you are sweating and begging for it, ready to give anything just to feel that rush as she plunges into you, the whole weight of her against you, your legs wrapped tight around her waist.

Still joined, you begin to sit up, tightening the muscles of your stomach as you push up against her. Your arms are around her as you kneel across her lap, kissing her neck, her chest, biting at the rounded curve of her shoulder as you ease her onto her back. She struggles against you, briefly, but then you are straddling her, riding her cock, your hands pressing into the floor on either side of her head as you lift yourself above her, getting just the right angle. You ride long and hard and fast, stopping and starting with utter abandon. The more you give yourself up the more she likes it, seeing you just let go, her decorous femme turned into a bitch in heat, sweat gleaming between your breasts as your neck arches back and your thighs shake with tension above her.

Sliding one arm around her waist, you press your hand against the dampness in the small of her back, cradling her to meet your mouth until all sense of time and space leaves you. Your brain is sparkling and popping like a match held to a box of fireworks. It doesn't matter that you told the bartender at the Lounge you'd be right back, that right this minute you should be stripping, go-go dancing, introducing a spoken-word show or whatever you'd planned for the night's entertainment at the club, because all the clichés are true. Truly nothing could make you stop, not now. You pull up and in and everything hangs poised on the crest of a wave, high and glittering, right *there*, until you come in a hot spurt all over her hands, pouring out hot over her legs and she grips you tight saying you're mine, you're mine and you answer yes, yes, all yours, and you're not thinking of Molly Bloom now, not even thinking at all, because finally you're not waiting, not waiting at all, in this moment you are exactly where you want to be.

C. Allyson Lee

Tribute to a Womyn Warrior

Babe. Superjock. Goddess. Poetry in motion. You are all of these things to me, and more. You stole my heart the day I first set eyes on you, and I've been lusting after you ever since.

You light up the ball field with your fresh, easy smile and that unmistakable infectious laughter. I'd love to play the field with you! You spread nothing but good, welcoming energy through the entire team, making each of us feel special. I love your thick, blue-black hair, shiny like a raven's coat, blowing in the wind and partly contained by your trusty baseball cap. Your eyes, on the rare times they're not hidden by sunglasses, are dark and intense, deep in concentration. You keep your firmly set jaw and your kissable neck straight and strong until you finally project the ball fiercely along its proper path.

I have wicked thoughts when I watch you stretch and warm up your magnificent body, with those perfectly shaped arms and legs. When you slip your hand into that dusty leather glove I find myself wishing I was that glove.

I know what it's like to be held by you in celebratory embrace, your arms encircling me affectionately and tightly every time we get someone out on base. You throw like a rocket, yet touch me so tenderly.

I love watching you at bat as you point your hot, tight butt towards me. Your gorgeous thighs spread out confidently, just enough to take control and show some attitude. When you hit one of your home runs it is pure ecstasy to see your powerful legs propel you around the diamond right up to that final slide into home plate. You do the splits like a gymnast, so effortless, so graceful. If only you would split like that for me in private!

I want to take you home, put you into a hot bubble bath, soak your aching coffee-coloured skin, stroke and soothe those tired muscles. Pat you dry, pamper and please you while you beg for more.

You are soft and slippery like warm rice noodles, as I adorn your loveliness with scented oil. I caress every inch of you with my fingertips in silent worship.

Not known for your shyness or passivity, you take. control. Taking my face in your piano player hands, you pull me down to meet your sweet lips. We catch fire. Your mouth opens onto mine and we hunger after each other, feeling hot breath on skin. I am sucking your lips and tongue. You taste like honey, feel like velvet, move like waves on the ocean. Exquisite kisser.

We are bathed in each other's wetness and heat.

I want you so badly it's unbearable. My hands move up and down your solid, smooth outline. I tingle at every curve and valley I discover.

I am overwhelmed by your roundness, hardness, lusciousness. I want to drink, lick and suck you dry.

My fingertips trace circles around your deliciously ripe breasts. I nibble each nipple, tease in and around them until your mocha button emerges, full and hard, like a cherry on top of a hot fudge sundae.

You grip my hair as I move my tongue downward to your hot little mound. I bury my face in your succulent fruit, my lips and tongue adore your precious jewel and work overtime. As I bask in the aroma of your dark folds, I am reminded of the steamy, delicate flavour and texture of shitake mushrooms.

Your fingers slide deeply into me as I try to pay attention to what I am doing. I flick the tip of my tongue relentlessly in and out of you, up, down and around your hot spot until your thighs clasp me like a vice. Your whole body shudders and you let out a scream so loud I think we've just had a grand slam.

But it's not over yet. I don't want to waste all that inviting cream you've given me. As you try to catch your breath I slip my fingers into you and quickly move in and out. You tell me to push harder. You plunge two, then three fingers into me. I grasp and clutch onto your hand wanting it to stay there forever. We writhe in unison and the reverberations are too much for me to bear. My entire being ripples as if electrified and we both scream as we collapse in each other's well-spent ardour.

The ultimate double play.

But alas, I am too shy to let you or anyone know I have impure thoughts about a team-mate and so am reduced to worship you from afar. I join the ranks of countless others, team-mates and spectators, who admire you. Warm, beautiful, sexy womyn of my dreams. My beloved Womyn Warrior.

JUDITH P. STELBOUM

Simple Lessons for Beginners

"Cut it out!" She pushed my arms away from her waist just before I grabbed her.

"Well," I smirked, "you wanted to know what two women do together."

"Yes...know...understand. I want you to explain it to me."

She still seemed interested but slightly awkward and nervous.

"Oh, I see, as in intellectual inquiry as opposed to experiential." I couldn't help laughing out loud because I knew what she really wanted. Me. I also knew she was scared to death and would never really make a move. So, how to play this? I mean we all come out some time, right? Right!

Although there is nothing in the official lesbian manual about transitions from friends to lovers, I know this must be one of the harder moments. I wished we had a real manual and promised to think about doing such a project.

So there we were, two Graduate Assistants sent by our

eastern university to the National Women's Studies Conference at a university in northern California. She was straight (I can hardly say that word without gagging). I was lesbian. We both taught Women's Studies, and the college, in all of its professional liberalism, had decided to be democratic and send one of each sex or gender, depending on your level of sophistication, philosophy and political correctness.

We sat in our room after dinner. It had been a rather stimulating day seeing all of the "stars of feminism" — famous scholars and writers — listening to the panels on "Goddess Imagery: An Artists' Symposium," "Cross Dressing: A Religious Perspective," "Feminism and the Case for Affirmative Action."

I decided to plunge ahead trusting my fate to the goddesses we had heard about earlier. We were far from home base and any lingering social or professional restrictions. The simple truth was I had just broken up a six-month affair and was feeling kind of loose and wild.

"You know, Tracy, it's hard to explain without some demonstration. Purely for clarity...that is."

She looked quizzically at me. I had to act fast. I didn't want her to doubt my sincerity. "I know you're a het all the way and I respect that as I know you respect me and my choice. That's why we're friends."

That was a good line, I thought. Stress the possibility of choices. What bullshit! How can you say such drivel to a friend? Well it's for a good cause. Right? Right.

"I know you wonder how two women get off without a penis. Isn't that it?" I didn't mention dildos. Too off-putting for the beginner.

I hoped I hadn't pushed too far. This was a delicate procedure and I hadn't had much practice. I wanted to tease her, tempt her. Oh crap, let's be honest. As soon as I thought there might be a glimmer of a possibility, fantasy time took over. I wanted to suck her, lick her, finger her, fuck her...the whole forty-nine yards. After all, it was only the first day of the conference and if everything worked out we could have three days of ecstasy instead of some more sessions on, "Were the Brontes Feminists?" or "Reverse Racism in *Their Eyes Were Watching God*."

Don't get cocky or superior, I warned myself and I quickly looked away from her gaze.

"Well...I guess I'm curious. I hope I don't make you uncomfortable by all these questions, Mickey, as if you were some specimen under a microscope."

My real name is Michelle but my friends call me Mickey. It has a dyke, butch ring to it which I like. Maybe the androgynous name would help. Maybe!

"Oh, no. We've been friends for a long time, Tracy, and I feel pretty easy with you. I'm happy to answer your questions. I'll have another glass of wine." She poured me some Almaden Red and I settled back into the club chair. "Shoot. What can I tell you?"

She was tentative. "Well, first you all seem to walk around smiling and grinning as if you had some secret no one else shared. What's that about?"

I slapped my free hand down on the chair arm. "So, you noticed." I laughed and shook my head.

"Well?"

She stood directly in front of me with her arms crossed. "Well what?"

"Well, what are you all always smiling at each other for? Moving so close? Whispering in each others ears? Always together in groups? How do you find each other anyway?"

"You know Tracy, that's a good question. How do you find them...us." I put my glass of wine on the table next to the chair. I raised my hand to my forehead and peered out, looking like an Indian Scout from an old western movie. "Many times I've wandered around looking, looking."

Tracy laughed. Then she dug her top teeth into her bottom lip and shook her head.

"Really, Tracy, It's hard to know. But here at the conference, it's a snap. Everyone feels pretty comfortable here and there's a lot of cruising going on. There's an atmosphere of potential possibility and we all know it. And," I whipped out my gold labyris which was a permanent fixture around my neck, "this is only one of the club members' signs, like the Elks or the Masons. When anyone sees the sign, well..." I chuckled and threw up my hands.

"And then what? What do you do then when you know or notice the signs?"

She poured herself another glass of wine.

"Oh, yeah. We're back to that." I pretended a shyness.

"Yes, we're back to that."

I like to think that in that moment, she really saw me for the first time in the two years we had known each other. I like to think she saw this tall, slim, olive-skinned dyke. My short curly hair cut so close it lay flat on my head so that sometimes people called me Mister or Sir.

I looked at her, too, but I had done this before. She had straight blonde hair that hugged her cheekbones. Her eyes were a light blue and her skin so white, I knew she could never be a sun worshipper. Sure I would like to run my hands down those full breasts. Open those legs and lay my face between them. I'd thought of it a few times, but always dismissed it as never happening. Why work myself into a state of disappointment? "You have to conserve your energy so your energy can serve you." I must've read that on some billboard back in New York. So conserve your energy, Mickey.

"Tracy, go sit down." I pointed to the chair next to the desk and some distance from me. "Just so there's no misunderstanding."

"Mickey, you're so funny. Are you scared of me?"

This was a new tack. Was she flirting? Maybe I could use it. "No, not scared. I just don't want to lose a good friend by doing something that might upset you."

She shook her head up and down but there was a different look in her eyes. Disappointment? Or was I projecting?

"Now, Mickey, if we take this step by step. First, there's kissing. I guess that's the same for me and you...the technique I mean, speaking clinically. The actual act itself."

I looked at her uncertainly. She just didn't get it.

She must've read my eyes. "And the feeling? Are you saying it's different when two women kiss?"

"I can only speak from my own experience, Tracy. When I kiss someone," I looked her straight in the eyes, "I feel it in my whole body. Breast against breast. Cunts together. Mouths open. It sets me tingling down here." I pointed to my cunt. "And it gets me soooo wet." I rubbed my hand over my warm crotch.

"I know where, Mickey. We are still both women." She sounded disgusted either with my simplicity or my grossness. Hard to say which. Actually, I had done it for effect. If I couldn't demonstrate on her, I could always use myself as a model.

"Well see, that's it." I leaned forward in the chair. "That's a big part of the excitement. You know what's happening with her body too. You know she's also getting wet. You know her nipples are getting as hard as yours. It's a big turn on."

"Oh, I never thought of it that way."

I decided now was the time to really push ahead. "Like

now, just talking about it, can you feel yourself getting a little moist?"

There was a silence before she asked, "More wine?"

I sensed that she was deciding whether to continue or end the analysis. It was a touchy moment. It could go either way depending on her fear or need. I knew the wine was in my favour but the hetero inhibition was strong.

"Sure, more wine." I held out my glass and didn't move. "Fill 'er up, babe."

She poured the wine in my glass and stood looking at me for a few seconds. I held her gaze and gave her what I hoped would be interpreted as a warm, affectionate, non-threatening smile. There was no sound except for some giggling from the adjoining room. She put the bottle on the table next to my chair. It felt as though everything in my life was balancing in this millisecond. She stood in front of the club chair and positioned herself between my open legs. I didn't dare break eye contact. I didn't even blink.

She lifted her hand and placed some fallen hair behind her ear. A nervous gesture, I thought. I had seen this gesture many times. Now it seemed so endearing, so sensual. I wanted to take that earlobe between my teeth, gnaw on it a little bit, lick that lobe and slowly stick my tongue into her ear. The giggling next door got louder. It was distracting.

"Must be some of *your* people." She nodded her head in the direction of the noise.

"Maybe." I relaxed even deeper into the chair. She was going to move. I knew it. She put both hands on my knees and leaned forward.

"Show me. Demonstrate. The kiss." She was smirking now.

I pulled back a little. What a tease. "For demonstration, right?"

She sat astride my legs, put her hand on the back of my neck and pulled me up towards her.

"Mickey, show me!"

Her eyes looked so soft and open, just like I knew she was going to be. Would she go all the way? I promised to rebuke myself later for my macho jock attitude. For now, there was only one way to find out.

I placed both my hands around her waist, held her close, stroked her back and ass and moved my fingers through her hair. Our mouths met and she closed her eyes. Her lips were soft and pliable. She kissed me back. It seemed as though it happened in slow motion, even though things moved pretty quickly.

She wore the kind of clothing I had rejected years ago. A full floral pattern skirt, white silk blouse, pantyhose, bra and slip. I had surreptitiously watched her dress this morning. Now feeling the loose fabric of the skirt under my palm, I was excited knowing I could just slide my hand up under her skirt and touch her. Suddenly, her outfit seemed so sexy. None of the women I'd been with dressed this way. We all seemed alike — Blazer Dykes.

"Oh, I like this." I ran my hand over her ass and lifted her skirt.

"You mean the skirt or what's under it?" She whispered into my ear.

"You're a fast learner." I bit her ear lobe. I bit her neck, then moved my mouth back to hers. We kissed deeply. She pushed her body closer into mine, and I realized she was following the manual guidelines I had mentioned a little while ago. I wondered if I should check for wetness. Yours or hers, I thought.

My hands moved up and just grazed the sides of her breasts. Even with a bra I knew she could feel that.

I heard her gasp as my thumbs agitated her nipples, back and forth. I could feel how hard they were through the blouse and bra. I moved the flat of my palms over her breasts and clasped them in my hands.

"Mickey."

"Mnnnnn." I still nibbled on her ear and moved down her neck with little bites, licks and kisses.

"Mickey?" She moved her head back out of range of my mouth and smiled at me. "Now what do you do?"

"Now? Now!" She forced me to stop. My heart was pounding, my jeans sticky and wet. I could smell my arousal. I managed to regain some composure and lightness. "Now you play it by ear!" We both grinned.

"Your bed or mine?" I motioned towards the two narrow twin beds.

"The nearest one." She laughed. "And you're right...I'm wet."

We were approaching another delicate moment...the disrobing. I didn't say what I was thinking but I was afraid that the vulnerability would be too much. I studied her closely. She seemed turned on. I proceeded to stage two and started to unbutton her blouse. She moved back into my arm to give me room. Ahh, a good sign. I grew bolder and bent to kiss her breasts held up by that restrictive bra. I touched them, squeezed them, hardening the nipples even more.

"Let me take it off." Her voice was raspy and insistent.

"God, oh, God." I put my face between them, pressing them into my cheeks and moved my mouth, teeth and tongue alternately over each delicious breast. They were so soft and so big with dark brown, delicate nipples. Each time I took a nipple in my mouth, I heard her gasp and felt her hips press into me.

"Tracy, I'm going to take off your skirt." I managed to voice between moans.

"I'll do it," she whispered so softly. I felt as if what we were doing was secretive.

As she let her skirt fall to the floor, I took off my shirt and pants. She sat on the bed and started in on her pantyhose.

"No." I stopped her hand at her waist and made no attempt to conceal the excitement in my voice. "No. Let me."

I gently pushed her back down on the bed. I was on my knees between her legs. My fingers touched the pantyhose along her waist, moved up and down the silky nylon of her calves, feet and thighs. I cupped my hand over her cunt and pressed down. Then moved my mouth between her thighs and breathed into her.

"Mickey...Mickey!"

There it was. I looked up and saw the panic in her eyes. She was losing control and was scared. I knew that's what it was because she loved it. Loved my touch, loved what she was feeling. I knew it. Oh, if only I had more practice with these situations. What to do? I was on my own, playing it by ear. Someone who plays by ear has to have an exquisite sensitivity to sound and touch. You have to switch quickly from one note to the next when you accidentally hit the wrong one.

I had two choices. Back off or be brave and trust in the intensity of her senses. That is, trust my sense of knowing where she was. It was the point of no return. I boldly pressed harder on her crotch, my hands stroking and kneading her breasts. I moved my palm over her clit and rubbed gently and slowly in small circles, alternating up and down with my index finger. It excited me even more to realize how wet she was but I knew I shouldn't say anything. It might frighten her even more. I started to remove her panty hose and noticed that I got some help as she raised her hips.

Now we were naked together. I slid on top of her. She seemed so passive but I accepted it as a beginner's hesitation and fear. I didn't really know what was going through her mind but I knew what was happening to her body.

"Tracy, Oh...oh...you're so wet," I couldn't stop myself from exclaiming as my index finger dipped between her legs and found her clit. "And so hard. God, your clit is so hard."

I could see the sides of her mouth turn upward into a small smile and then her lips parted. "Yes."

That was it. The go ahead. The green light. The beckoning finger, the winking eye. It was all I needed. I knew she would go all the way with me. I could feel my own wetness seep out of me. I wanted to rub it on her face to show her how she affected me. I stopped myself thinking it would probably be too much for a beginner. Instead I spread my legs over her thigh and rubbed up and down.

"I'm so wet, too, baby. You make me so wet. You're beautiful."

I pinched her nipples, squeezed those large, soft breasts and moved my hand down again to her wet cunt.

I could hear her quiet gasps and moans as she tried to control her responses.

"It'll give, baby. Don't worry. Relax. You'll get it. Just play it by ear." I gushed.

Now was the moment to enter her. It was what she was used to and I was curious about her reaction to fingers. Maybe we could discuss this later when in a cooler state. After all, I mean, we were at a conference.

She spread her legs for my probing hand and in a rough, low voice surprised me.

"Inside. Go inside me."

I slid first one, two, then three fingers inside her. Oh god, she was like silk. Slick and wet. Pulsating. I moved my fingers, twisted them inside her, rubbed and touched those wondrous walls. I felt every motion and stroke inside my own cunt.

"Oh, oh, oohhh." Her hands grabbed the headboard, holding on tight...but I wasn't having any of this so fast. I slowed my motion down to a standstill and moved lower on her belly.

I was ready to dare it all, now. How would she respond to the next stage? I lifted my head from her belly and looked at her face. Her eyes were closed. Her cheeks were flushed. Her head was slowly moving from side to side.

I inhaled the essence of this woman. Oh, she was so sweet and tangy all at once. I moved my tongue lightly. She jumped and jerked as if some electric shock went through her. My fingers again moved inside her and I slowly rubbed my tongue up and round her clit just lightly touching the sensitive opening.

Her body bucked so hard, I had to pin her to the bed with my shoulders. I listened to her tremulous, inarticulate sounds. Her fingers pushed my head deeper into her.

She was so close now. I was too. I kept the rhythm. Inexorable. That's what one of my lovers had said. You can't escape it, get away from it. It takes you like an ocean wave, picks you up and carries you over. And that's what I wanted to do to her, for her. Carry her over to the other side. Show her what it was like. What it could be like. The reason for all those smiles and giggles.

Suddenly, she inhaled deeply and exploded. The screams surely enlightened the gigglers next door and all the women who slept a few floors below and above us. The shudders came and came.

"Don't...don't...don't...stop."

Her hand held mine, or should I say clamped over mine and held me inside her while her other hand pushed my head away from her clit.

Sweat covered her body. I lay on top of her. I heard her heart pound and felt the contractions deep inside still responding to my hand. I couldn't help an involuntary jerk or two myself in response to what she was experiencing.

I kissed her. She stuck out her tongue to lick my cheeks and lips.

"I love the way you taste." I said.

She smiled. "Mmnnn."

When I slipped my fingers out, I could see the loss reflected in her expression. "Aarrgh. No!" Her body arched and withdrew. She seemed so disappointed.

Minutes later she opened her eyes.

"You're terrific." I said. I looked into her eyes and smoothed back some blonde hair clinging to her damp forehead.

"You're a great teacher."

"No," I responded in my best academic tone. "A teacher is only as good as her students, and you're a great student."

"Beginner's luck." She grinned.

CLAIRE ROBSON

Please Wear Romantic Attire

I checked the address on the Valentine party invitation one last time before I folded the red card and crammed it into my pocket, no doubt breaking or at least bruising some of the little pink hearts which decorated it.

"Please Wear Romantic Attire." At least my underpants qualified. They were a brief snatch of black lace, cut down just below the start of my pubic hair and crested with a pearl. Almost everything else was black leather. The trousers were tight, though not uncomfortable, curving around my buttocks and firmly holding my crotch. Pip had bought me the cowboy boots for my birthday, and the left one flaunted a set of silver chains. The tiny Native American vest exposed my back, arms, shoulders and the tops and sides of my breasts clutched in a glimpse of taut black leather. My shirt was black cotton, with victorian leg of mutton sleeves and a demure little row of buttons right up the front.

The jewellery I chose was all silver, a thick dog chain and

a slender one for contrast, a heavy earring in my left ear, and on the right middle finger a broad ring depicting two dolphins entwined in an embrace.

Just before we left, I pulled on my jacket. It was Pip's first Christmas present to me and my most treasured possession. All the leather we have since added to my collection has been modelled on the jacket's soft, thick, jet-black shine. It cuts away to the waist but curves around my breasts and shoulders. It has short zips down the back and at the cuffs. I have only to put on this jacket to rise to the challenge of looks and glances which black leather attracts.

The party was professional, wealthy and delicate. The couple who hosted it were as nervous and attentive as any other aspiring suburban pair. I was amazed to find they not only had a champagne cooler but also a hired help who removed glasses as soon as they were put down and discreetly replenished the plates of creamy little desserts as fast as they were consumed. As I engaged in polite conversation with the socially easy and munched happily through flakey confections that collapsed and oozed in my mouth, I assessed appearances. Our hostesses were elegant — Louise in a loosely cut jacket and skirt and Pat in a crisp white blouse, severe black skirt and red rose. There were other variations on the theme of "Romantic Attire," from matching t-shirts ("I'm Charlene's Girl"/"I'm Sally's Girl") to shirts with red hearts.

I have noticed that people react in varied ways when I wear black leather. In bars, some women ask to touch it. Some women turn the other way. Some assume a flirtatious air of mock submission, and others add an almost imperceptible edge to their manner. At this party, no one reacted very much at all, until the very end, when Pip, who loves to challenge me in public, suggested that I take off my shirt. I have learned from experience that the only way to retain any dignity when Pip makes these suggestions is to act promptly.

As I undid the short row of buttons at the front and slipped off the cotton shirt, I was unaware of the crowded room behind me, until an arm crawled playfully around my leg. I turned to meet a concerted and admiring stare. The combination of my well-defined arm and shoulder muscles, tight black leather, alcohol and the spirit of St. Valentine produced a palpable wave of sexual energy in the room. As I turned away, rather confusedly, to say goodbye to someone who was leaving, she reached out and stroked my arm gently.

"Nice deltoids," she murmured.

Out of the corner of my eye I saw Pip's sardonic smile.

We left shortly afterwards and when we got home I went into the bedroom and pulled off my boots. Next I peeled off my trousers, folded them and set them carefully beside the boots. As I considered taking off my black lace panties and the vest, Pip looked around the door.

"Leave that on 'til I get back from the bathroom," she said casually.

When she came back, she began to play with me gently, stroking the black leather vest, pulling the fringes and examining the way my breasts bulged against the top. She rolled me onto my stomach and untied the strap that held the vest together. It came away in her hands as I turned and tried to kiss her. Pushing me firmly back onto the bed, she untied the two chains around my throat and ran the chill metal slowly across my belly. Then she turned her attention to my nipples.

She took my right nipple firmly between her fingers and twisted it 'til it swelled and stiffened. She coiled the heavy chain in a spiral around my breast, pulling it tightly so that it sank into the softness. Then she squeezed breast and chain together with both hands leaving the nipple straining to be touched. She leaned down and put her tongue to it, then raised her head to look at my reaction.

"That's so good," I said. "I want you to do it harder."

She gave my breast a rough squeeze, and examined the way it made my aching nipple stand up still further before she took it between her lips. Her other hand strayed to my other breast, then grabbed it. She fumbled 'til she found that nipple too, and trapped it, squeezing and twisting breast and nipple together. Meanwhile, her teeth had replaced her lips at the first nipple, nibbling and teasing it. I opened my legs wide, rolling my hips and hoping she would touch me, but she only smiled and picked up the heavy dog chain in her left hand. Her right hand began to rub the hairs at the top of my pubis. As she looked into my eyes, she slid her fingers down the outside of my soaked panties and brought them to my face for me to smell. She pulled my panties down and off and pushed my legs apart again, with a hand on each knee. Casually, she licked her lips.

Parting my wet and sticky hairs, she flicked her tongue over my clitoris. I jerked and shuddered as she slowly pulled the chain up and across the slit of my vagina...hot wet tongue and chill sharp chain together.

"So, you like this, do you?"

"Yes, yes, oh god..."

I was at the point of orgasm when suddenly she was on top of me. Her hands clutched my buttocks as she rode me, giving me just enough to keep me gasping. I could feel the heat of her against my leg. As we both came near to fusion we slowed and stopped. I rolled off her t-shirt, stroked and fondled a hanging breast in each hand, licked and sucked the tightness of her nipples, forcing her to press her in-flamed sex against me again. After a few minutes, she took my wrists and forced them above my head. Picking up the leather vest, she blindfolded me and went to work on my nipples again, wrapping the chain around each of them in turn, twisting it to the point where pain and pleasure min-gle. Forcing and squeezing my breasts together so that my nipples nearly touched she was able to pass quickly from one to the other, biting and sucking, holding both breasts in one hand in order to fuck me with the vibrator. She let me feel its snub nose seeking entrance before she sank it deep into me, plunging it again and again, all the while kneading and teasing my tits harder and harder. I felt her lips at my neck, and moved in a way I knew excited her, until she took hold of me in her teeth, growling softly with pleasure.

Finally she left the vibrator inside me and kissed me, filling my willing mouth with her salty tongue, reminding me that while others might look, I want only her to take me like this.

Lifting the blindfold and slipping out the vibrator, I rolled her onto her back and took up position above her. My knees were on either side of her head, my hands were fumbling with her panties. I moistened her swollen clitoris by smearing it with the flood I felt between the folds of her labia then rolled it gently between my thumb and finger and caught the same rhythm on the breast and nipple I held in the other hand. She entered me again from below, a mute appeal for the same attention on my part. When I lost count of the fingers she was pumping into my dripping wet slit with the same insistent beat I was using on her clitoris, I rolled her round 'til we were side by side. I slid down to make the most of her hot wet cunt, inhaling her, teasing my fingers at the edge of her vagina until she forced herself over and around me, then rewarding her with the hard insistent pressure of my tongue, the sly relentless movement of my fingers, bringing her to the edge, then slowing just enough to keep her hanging there, pinned to my touch.

Carefully, I slid my fingers out, using them to rub her clitoris in a firm circular motion, moving my mouth to hers, my other hand to her breast, holding her on the very brink of orgasm. Moving my body onto her, clutching her shoulders to drive my hips into her, feeling her shudder, hearing her moan, I was driven by the same wild unstoppable joy of knowing that in five, six, seven strokes more we would explode. I drew her to me, wrapping my arms around her and as our mouths fastened together we were rocked by the same blast. We clutched each other as if for protection from its force, as if we expected clouds of dust, debris, pieces of masonry.

Later, we reoriented ourselves in the bed, plumped the pillows and set the alarm. Pip fished out her pyjamas, decorated with indeterminate animals on skis. I struggled into my oversized t-shirt, which pronounces me a member of the teddy club.

"Romantic attire," I murmured softly as we snuggled together in our wet patch, but she was already asleep.

JANA WILLIAMS

All's Fair

Zanzi stretched out the full length of the contour chair in the lobby of the clubhouse. She crossed her legs at the ankles and stared out the wide expanse of window that previewed the exterior of the park. Occasionally, her golden eyes flickered to the wide door at the entrance to the building, or the double doors that led to the gymnasium and showers.

She had no idea what the woman she was waiting for looked like. She chuckled to herself as she stretched languorously. She had flown across the continent by hydrojet, risked calling a total stranger to invite her to a contest in an unsown erospark, and then forgotten a basic essential. By forgetting to ask how she would recognise her, Zanzi had spent a certain amount of time and energy thinking, dreaming, imagining her. Maybe too much time. Zanzi rolled her eyes in self-reproach and promptly smiled an acquittal. It had been fun trying to construct an image purely from the impulses she had received from the woman's voice. Zanzi sighed, at least she knew her name. Meta. Meta Ampearse.

Friends in Yorksphere had insisted that if she were flying to SouSec, she must visit the erospark. It was rumoured to be one of the oldest in existence, and still one of the best. Zanzi's eyes roamed the interior of the clubhouse, it was interchangeable with any of the others which she had visited. The double doors that led to the gym shushed open and two women, striding shoulder to shoulder, pushed through. Their gym bags swung rhythmically as they walked. Zanzi's eyes followed them appreciatively. There was something about South Sector women.

After she had boarded the hydrojet in Yorksphere, she received one final transmission in her earpiece before the air lock sealed all communication with the ground. Her friends had said, "And when you get to SouSec, call Meta Ampearse; she'll make sure you have a good time at the erospark. Win or lose." The transmission had ended in a conspiratorial giggle. Zanzi had been tempted to shrug it off. But as the hydrojet disgorged it's passengers in SouSec she found herself rising to the challenge that had been implicit in her friends parting. What harm could it do to locate Meta while she was here?

When Zanzi had finally contacted her, Meta's voice in her earpiece had been cool, controlled, self-assured with just a hint of the sector accent that the computer chip couldn't erase. Zanzi got the impression that it wasn't all that unusual for Meta to field calls from total strangers who wanted to explore the southern sector's erospark. Zanzi had no sooner transmitted her proposal on her earpiece and mentioned several references in Yorksphere, when Meta went under. The micro computer in Zanzi's ear that simultaneously translated, transmitted and received thought patterns on prearranged frequencies, had gone blank. Zanzi finished unpacking, knowing that Meta's voice would resurface once she had accessed a frequency booster and checked the references Zanzi had mentioned.

Zanzi was in the midst of her daily swim, several hours later, when Meta's voice wove itself into her movements. As usual with earpieces, the more concentrated Zanzi was in what she was doing, the more garbled was the reception. Once she remembered to turn over on her back and float while conversing, Meta's voice came in loud and clear. It was delightful accompaniment to her swim. Their earlier conversation had been somewhat cool, even aloof. Now, there was a current of interest warming the woman's low voice. Zanzi lay back and let the pool water wash over her. She closed her eyes and listened as Meta's husky voice described the erospark and the peninsula on which it was located. Zanzi frog-kicked lazily and the rush of warm water over her bare breasts was seductive as a lover's caress. Meta's voice throbbed like a song. Zanzi found herself replying in contented "ummms" and "uh huhs."

Suddenly, in the mist of one of Meta's thought transferences, Zanzi bolted upright in the pool. As her feet found the bottom of the pool she blurted aloud, "In the name of Medusa." This was psychological seduction of the most blatant kind and she had nearly let herself float right into it. It was obvious that Meta was prepared to start the contest right now and would use any number of ruses to achieve her own end. A slow smile spread across Zanzi's face. Well...that was alright. It had been a long time since anyone in Yorksphere had felt like much of a challenge. Once she had regained her composure, Zanzi had reconnected with Meta's frequency.

"Sorry, I lost some of your transmission there. So, we'll meet tomorrow at middle a.m.? Okay. Great. See you then."

That was when she had neglected to ask how she would recognise Meta.

The clubhouse door opened. Zanzi looked up at the sound and watched a small, square woman step across the threshold. Her black, curly hair was windblown and she wore the darkened eyeshades nearly all southern sector natives had adopted. She advanced towards Zanzi with her gym bag slung over one shoulder. Her smile was brilliant, her thoughts transmitted with certainty, "Zanzi." Meta Ampearse extended her free hand.

Zanzi firmly grasped Meta's hand, but took some time to rise from the chair. The game had already begun and she was aware that she must plan each move carefully. In the moments before she rose, Zanzi appraised her opponent. Meta was firm and compact, her hands were small and fine-boned. She moved with a definite lightness that seemed born of self-assurance. The preciseness of her movements hinted of an underlying strength. The same could be said of her shoulders. Her skimpy singlet exposed soft, supple skin. The pulse beating at the base of Meta's throat begged to be kissed. As she swung her gym bag back over her shoulder, her muscles knotted and relaxed. Everything about the woman screamed contradictions. Zanzi knitted her brow struggling to keep her thoughts to herself.

Meta shoved her bag beneath Zanzi's chair. "This should be safe here. Shall we go check in?" Zanzi rose in consent. She was easily a full head taller than Meta, and more muscled. Zanzi's legs were long, with well-defined calves, square knees and finely muscled thighs. Meta's eyeshades made it impossible to verify but Zanzi could feel the intuitive tickle of Meta's own appraising glance.

At the registration counter, they held their thumbs to a darkened identity screen. It glowed green, then yellow as a computer flashed their names and time of arrival across the glass. They waited while the computer activated their files. A hollow beep indicated that they were cleared to pass through the gate.

In an alcove beside the door to the park was a stunning array of shelves. The contents were the latest in erospark play toys. Dildoes were lined like soldiers in a phalanx of erections that far exceeded mother nature's wildest imaginings. A slender fibreglass mannequin had cock rings encircling both arms up to her elbows. Behind it shelves were laden with gels, lotions, paints and salves. Nearest the door was a final, incredible display of sexwithes at which Zanzi halted.

"Didn't you bring your own withe?" Meta asked.

"No. The energy cell went on the fritz just before I left Yorksphere." Zanzi replied. "It's sitting in the repair shop at my club. I've been thinking of trying one of the new pulsating models."

They both fell silent as they inspected the various sexwithes. The newest models were equipped with triggers that sent a pulsating wave of energy from the tip of the withe. Focus rings allowed the user to send a broad band of energy on one setting or a narrow, more intense band on another. Of course, all the sexwithes could still be used in direct contact with the body. Their humming energy cells kept them at body temperature and produced a low-level vibration that was easily integrated into sexual play.

Zanzi selected a deep amber coloured pulsating model with a variable focus ring. She tested its feel in her hand. For a shelf model its balance was quite good, the handle was just about the right size and the wrist strap was adjustable. She said as much to Meta and passed it over to her for her inspection.

"Yeah, you're right. It's nice. They seem to be paying a lot more attention to detail on mass production designs these days." Meta handed her own withe to Zanzi. "I had this one made a couple of years ago. It was state-of-the-art then."

"It's beautiful." Zanzi inspected the withe. It fit neatly in her palm, with the trigger just where her index finger curled around the handle. Obviously Meta's hands were bigger than they looked, Zanzi mused. "Is this a real wood handle?"

"Umm. Nice isn't it." Meta crooned. She looked up from examining the new sexwithe Zanzi had taken off the shelf. "Look, why don't you use my withe this time? I mean, here you are at a strange park and having to use a production model withe as well." She smiled coyly. "It would seem that I have all the advantages. Let's even it up a bit."

Zanzi searched Meta's face, but the ever-present eyeshades made her expression unreadable. She sounded sincere. Zanzi shook her head and handed Meta her own withe. "No, no, that's too generous of you."

"I insist." Meta pushed the wand back into Zanzi's hands. "You use mine. I'll take the untried shelf model."

Not to be outdone by Meta's gallantry, Zanzi nodded in acceptance. She cradled the lovely withe, testing it's weight in her hand. "It's a pity you can't try out that shelf model to get a feel for just how accurate its focus might be."

"Oh, I'm sure it will be fine," Meta shrugged.

"Still, its a shame not to know how accurate the scatter focus is compared to the nucleated setting." Zanzi wasn't entirely sure that Meta had heard her. She appeared to be completely involved in fussing with the focus ring on the new withe.

"Ummm. It is a shame." Meta's right hand grasped the

withe, her index finger curling and uncurling near the trigger. Her left thumb and forefinger toyed with the focus ring. Slowly, very slowly, Meta's right index finger contracted, as the withe tip centred on Zanzi's solar plexus. In a halo of light the energy beam left the sexwithe and leaped the short distance between the two women. Zanzi was struck in the very same moment that she became aware of what Meta was intending.

With no time to prepare, Zanzi was a sitting duck. The energy beam hit her just above her navel. Immediately, undulating waves of longing rippled through her whole body. Goose bumps marched across the skin of both of Zanzi's arms. Her nipples became attentive and erect. As the energy beam churned through the lower half of her body, Zanzi's legs became useless. They were so weak and wobbly that if Meta had chosen to fire again Zanzi couldn't have been able to avoid it.

Zanzi gritted her teeth and forced her mind to stop it's wild imaginings. It was not Meta's hands that were skipping across her thighs. It was only the energy from the withe. It was not Meta's bold, beautiful mouth fashioning delirious designs across her breasts and abdomen. Zanzi watched helplessly as a slow smile spread across Meta's face.

Meta lowered her eyeshades slightly and drawled. "I'd say this withe works well enough." She turned abruptly and headed for the door to the park. "Catch me, if you can."

Zanzi was incapable of moving and could only sputter, "You...you cheat." She forced herself to breathe deeply. She must rid her thoughts of all images of Meta, or even the revenge she would soon extract. Right now, her priority was to counter the effects of the sexwithe. Zanzi understood that like any other sex toy, the magic of the withe was mostly in her mind. The most advanced sex toy in the world could only build, only heighten feelings that were already in existence. If there was any sublimated desire a sexwithe would expose it. If used properly, that desire could be intensified and refined into any number of games to be played over and over again.

Finally, her limbs returned to normal. Zanzi cleared her head enough to begin planning her next course of action. She stopped long enough to let her microchip scan Meta's frequency. If she was persistent she would soon begin to receive clues to Meta's location within the park. Of course there was the chance that the clues might be a ruse of Meta's meant to lure Zanzi into a trap. On the other hand, she might be able to decode them and construct an ambush of her own. Zanzi consulted a map of the park trails and connected open spaces that was displayed just outside the door.

From the map and the clues she began to receive in her earpiece, Zanzi deduced that Meta was heading along the trail that followed the beach. There was a longer trail, through the woods, that led to the same rendezvous. Zanzi immediately loped off in the direction the map had indicated. She might be able to outrun Meta and arrive at the beach clearing first. Her longer stride and the packed smooth surface of the higher trail would be to her advantage. Zanzi was counting on the fact that Meta would be hindered by the loose sand along the beach; but then, Meta knew the park well.

A mere hundred yards along the trail, a dense mass of green on each side completely blocked any view of the clubhouse behind her. Zanzi pushed herself to find, and hold, a running rhythm. The trail curled in a long tendril up a slight slope. Zanzi imagined it ending on a small bluff that over looked the sea. Deep in thought, she was planning her impending strategy when an irregular motion in the brush, an unexpected flash of colour and some sixth sense warned her, and she dropped instantly to one knee on the trail. The warming beam of a sexwithe sizzled near her shoulder. A burst of brilliant blue coloured the air around her. Zanzi glanced up just in time to see Meta disappear around a leafy bend in the trail.

With a sprinter's grace Zanzi streaked after Meta. Around the bend, the trail broadened into a meadow that carpeted a slight slope to the beach and then the sea. Zanzi halted to survey the open area. No sign of Meta. A stream near the tree line bordered the meadow on the left and lazily emptied into the ocean. Zanzi hurried for cover under the tree line. She crept along its edge, scouring the shadows and thickets. Her mind probed Meta's thought frequency. Quiet. Good, that meant Meta was nearby and was doing every-thing she could to block transmission. Suddenly, before her mind could really even process thought, Zanzi's eyes caught a flash of bare leg. Zanzi intuitively pointed the sexwithe and fired. Meta sprang from the underbrush only yards ahead of Zanzi and collapsed in a delayed reaction to the sexwithe's energy beam.

Smiling broadly, Zanzi strolled boldly towards the pros-trate Meta. This had been almost too easy, she told herself. With one toe she poked the sole of Meta's boot. Meta's back arched in orgasm and Zanzi threw back her head and laughed at the moan that escaped Meta's lips. Slowly Meta rolled over and Zanzi looked down at her prize, ready to lend her a hand to get to her feet. With clam determination Meta unloaded the full contents of her own sexwithe, which she had concealed beneath her body.

"You *fake.*" Zanzi roared as she felt the strength in her legs slip away and she slowly crumpled on to the grass next to Meta. In a final act of desperation she grasped Meta and pulled her close. Meta resisted, and as they wrestled they began to roll down the grassy slope together. Half way to the bottom their mingled laughter bound them as intimately as their intertwined arms and legs.

As they stopped rolling, Zanzi hauled herself atop Meta and kissed her smiling lips. Meta's hands gripped Zanzi's hair, her tongue tunnelled deeply into Zanzi's mouth. She felt Meta's body arch beneath her in an attempt to turn them over. Meta's strength surprised, then aroused Zanzi further. She threw her weight onto Meta's torso, pinning her to the ground. Zanzi sank her teeth into the soft skin behind Meta's ear, at first biting gently and then harder as Meta moaned in response. Meta grasped Zanzi's buttocks with both hands and pressed and kneaded the flesh until Zanzi gasped.

Shifting her weight to one side, Zanzi used one hand to explore Meta's body. She slipped her fingers under the waistband of Meta's singlet. At the same time Zanzi began to rub herself against Meta's thigh. Slowly she searched the mound of Meta's pubic hair, stroking the labia that was now wet. The skin of Meta's upper thighs was soft; softer than twilight. Finally, deliberately, Zanzi's fingers found Meta's clitoris. Buried with the dark swirls of hair it waited, rigid in anticipation.

Meta pulled Zanzi's mouth onto hers again as Zanzi slid her fingers then her palm over Meta's pubis. She rubbed slowly, then faster and harder until Meta was gasping for release. When she came, it was with a low guttural moan, her mouth pressed tightly against Zanzi's neck. The sound of Meta's orgasm triggered Zanzi's own. Meta pressed Zanzi tightly to her, continuing to rock her against her thigh even after Zanzi was unable to do so herself. The orgasm stretched into oblivion.

For what seemed like hours, they lay collapsed onto each other, their breathing synchronized and their bodies limp. Zanzi lay with her face pressed into Meta's neck and felt, rather than saw, the smile that spread across Meta's face. Zanzi felt laughter gather in the body beneath her. She raised her head to look into Meta's eyes and encountered, once again, the damnable eyeshades. Carefully, Zanzi lifted them and discovered her lover's eyes, brown as coffee, and flecked with fathomless laughter.

"You win." Meta whispered.

JOANNIE BRENNAN

Control

Legs bent at the knees and ankles securely tied to opposite bed posts, she arched against the tongue that probed and teased. The clamps that gripped her nipples had hurt at first but now were raising her to a higher plane of excitement. Her hands in their padded restraints clutched only air, bound as they were to the bed frame. Her eyes saw only the inside of her own mind. No light penetrated her blindfold. Her sensations were limited to the tongue on her cunt and the clamps on her nipples. The lack of distraction condensed and focused what she could feel until she wondered if she'd be able to stand the intensity for much longer. She held on. Her breathing quickened and became ragged as she felt the dildo at the rings that fringed her cunt and then slid in to nestle deeply inside her. The tongue quickened its pace, dancing down on her abdomen, holding her to the mattress as she felt the first waves of her orgasm start.

"Now," she cried out hoarsely. The shock of the double

needles, left and right, swooped sudden and sure, through the clamps and through her nipples.

She screamed as the pain added its intensity to her orgasm. A few minutes later, when her breathing had quietened, the piercer asked gently, "May I put the rings in now?"

She merely nodded.

KISS & TELL

Edmonton

I saw Her again in a bar in Edmonton.

I was there with a strange mix of university students, granola dykes, and leather girls who were looking after Kiss & Tell while we were in town. The bar was mostly men, mostly in couples, loud juke-box, small dance floor. It was a quiet night, but every night was a quiet night. I didn't care. If we had been in Vancouver, everyone would have been complaining — what a dead night, this is boring, let's go to the Shaggy, Ms. T's, anywhere else but here.

If we were in Vancouver the butch bottom in the chain-link vest wouldn't have been caught dead dancing with the scrub-cheeked grad student, laughing and bouncing up and down to the music, so uncool. But this was Edmonton.

It was a Euro crowd, with the exception of a tall thin East Asian fag who danced like a performance artist, and a South Asian dyke professor with long black hair and an English accent who was sitting across the table from me.

I was talking to a femme who seemed to belong to the

dancing chainlink butch (or vice versa, more likely). She was fat and smart and knew all about local politics. She kept a casual eye on the dance floor, not like she needed to worry about any sweetfaced academic, but more like she was enjoying the view.

"Three gay bashings in one day," she was saying. "That's what lesbian and gay visibility means in Alberta."

The dyke professor leaned across to us.

"And it's no wonder, with the fine example our government sets. First they say gays have more rights than anyone else, when we're not even covered by the human rights code! And now they're talking about restricting immigration — only English-speaking people need apply."

"Why do you stay?" I asked.

"We should just leave?" asked the femme. "We should just give the province to the Aryan Nation?"

"And where would I go?" asked the professor. "To your fine province where feminist professors receive death threats and nothing is done about it?"

"Yes, but Alberta is...well, you know...everyone talks about it like it's worse," I offered lamely.

The professor sighed. "Perhaps it is. Or maybe it's just a convenient place for the rest of the country to feel superior to."

She took a swig of her beer. I took a swig of my mineral water. We contemplated Alberta. The bar was starting to fill by now and the air was thick with smoke. The chainlink butch stopped by our table long enough to give her girl a squeeze before going back to dancing. The music was still relentlessly middle-of-the-road disco.

"Don't look now, but there's someone staring at you," said the femme.

"Me? Who? Where?"

"Over there at that table with all the flannel shirts."

I looked. Then I looked again. It was Her. That Woman. The one who fucked me over (and over and over) in Halifax. And she was staring at me.

I looked away, confused. It couldn't be Her. She was three thousand miles away. And she looked different. Her hair was the wrong colour. Her face was the wrong shape. She was too thin. It had to be someone else.

But it was Halifax. I recognized the eyes, the angle of her head, the way she sat, arms crossed, legs spread.

The femme smirked. "Maybe she wants your autograph."

"No. I know her." I looked again. She was still staring.

"Oh god," I said.

"Is that 'Oh god,' like we should scare her off, or 'Oh god,' like we should gracefully fade and tell your friends you won't be back tonight?"

"I don't know! I thought I'd never see her again," I said.

The professor shook her head sadly. "Our friend seems a bit incoherent. Perhaps she needs some help."

They pulled me out of my chair and shoved me toward the table where Halifax was sitting.

She looked good in a flannel shirt. Some girls do.

"Hi," I said.

She stared at me. So did the other women at her table. So much for prairie hospitality.

"Um, remember me?" Not a great opening line for an almost famous artist from the big city.

The women at the table looked away.

"I met you in Halifax?" my voice squeaked. I probably sounded desperate. I was making a fool of myself. Maybe it wasn't her.

But it was her. She glanced at me and looked away. The other women shifted nervously.

"Well, uhh…see you around," I said, trying for nonchalance

and failing. She was studying her thumbnail. She had lovely bitten cuticles. She was a jerk. Fuck her. The professor looked away, as if she hadn't just watched me be humiliated by a table of flannel shirts, which of course she had. Damn. I walked out of the bar. It seemed like a good idea at the time.

It was late-night downtown; empty streets, locked doors, stars rioting in the big Alberta sky. I crossed on a red light. Rebel rebel. Maybe I'd walk all night. Maybe I'd run into k.d. lang and she'd take me home. But she lives in Langley now, not Alberta. Maybe I'd get the bus back to my hotel room.

I heard footsteps, faint at first, about a block behind me. Hah! She *did* remember me. I wasn't going to turn around. No way. I could play hard to get too. I heard more footsteps. Did she bring all her flannel friends? Maybe it was just some lost tourists, looking for a midnight mall. I sped up a little. So did the footsteps. I looked over my shoulder, casual like. Their shaved heads gleamed under the street lights. Damn.

There were five or six of them, skinny white boys walking in a tight pack, their gangling adolescent grace transformed to a threat on this dark street. I sped up. The skinheads sped up. I crossed the street. They crossed after me. There wasn't an open store on the whole block. Fuck Edmonton on a Saturday night. I turned the corner and someone grabbed me.

"Come on!" she whispered and pulled me into a run, down the block and into an alley. The boys were out of sight around the corner, but I could hear them shouting and running after us. Without hesitating she leaped onto a parked car, clambered up a ladder of steel rungs conveniently set into the side of the building, onto the flat roof, and out of sight.

"Gee, she must really know Edmonton," I thought as I flung myself after Her.

When I reached the roof, I tripped over her in the darkness and she pulled me down on top of her.

"Ssshhhh," she hissed.

Down below I could hear the skinheads reach the end of
the alley and fade away. I was suddenly acutely aware of
my position and rolled off of her. This put me a little too
close to the edge of the roof, but it seemed safer, somehow,
than lying on top of Her.

"They're gone," I whispered.

"For now."

We lay there, listening. The dark silhouettes of other
buildings rose around us and the stars burned overhead.
The roof smelled of tar paper and prairie air. Halifax moved
closer, running her hand along my arm. I could smell her. I
remembered how she had touched me in that coffee bar
washroom. I remembered how abruptly she had left. "No,"
I said. Her hand hesitated. "We have to talk."

"Okay," she said. "What do you want to talk about?"

"What do I want to talk about?" I sat up. It's a better
position for indignation. "Well, let's start with where did
you go? Why did you just disappear? Who the hell are you,
anyway? And what the fuck are you doing *here*?"

"Saving your ass," she said sweetly.

That stopped me. I had forgotten to be grateful. Damn.
I was trying to stutter out my thanks when she lunged at
me and pulled me down beside her, her hand over my
mouth. I kicked at her and tried to squirm out of her grip,
but she held me.

Then I froze. I could hear the soft footfalls in the alley
below, the half-whispered words of the skinheads. There
was a sudden clang of metal on metal. A cat screamed. Then
silence.

Her body was warm next to mine. I pressed against her.

"Shit," I whispered.

"Ssshhh," she replied, her hot breath in my ear.

The skinheads were whispering again, closer, then further away. I could follow their voices as they moved methodically from one end of the alley to the other, searching. She held me close, one hand moving down my back, searching. I pushed it away. She stopped. My ass felt cold where her hand had been. I put it back, and felt silent laughter on my cheek.

The boys were getting louder, laughing at jokes I couldn't hear. The occasional word floated up from the alley — screw, bitch, kill. She kissed my throat, my eyes, my mouth, pausing to undo a few buttons, and a few more. The night air licked my breasts. Her hands were hot and hard on my hard nipples. The skinheads were yelling. I was moaning, muffling my mouth in her neck, tasting her salt skin.

There was a loud crash below, then another.

"Garbage cans," she breathed into my ear. "They're trashing the alley."

In my mind's eye I could see the sounds, cans kicked, rolling away, spilling garbage. Her arms were around me, silent, defiant. Her smell filled me. I clung to her, biting her neck, her lips, rocking against her blue-jeaned cunt. She held me, open, yearning. Her hands slow, deliberate, undeniable, on my thighs. Her mouth. Her hips. She undid me, found me, wet and desperate. The sound of breaking glass, store windows, car windows. My cunt was huge, swollen. It filled the sky. Her slow strokes filled me, forced me open, open, holding me gasping on the edge of helpless powerful breaking like glass falling the stars screaming silence breaking, my fingers twisted in her flannel shirt.

EVE HARRIS

True Story

This is a true story, a true story and just like Nardo Ranks',
it has an Indian girl with long black hair and light brown
skin. She was standing in the 14th Street subway station on
the uptown side. She was all the way at the north end,
leaning against the grey bin, reading a magazine. I was on
the downtown side, waiting for the train to Brooklyn, when
I saw her.

I had seen her before, a few months ago. I had been
outside this Western shop on Hudson Street, looking at a
pair of cowboy boots and all of a sudden there was a
brilliant red glare on the store window. I looked over my
shoulder and saw her, a pretty, caramel-skinned girl in a red
fur coat. She was staring at me, but I didn't think I could
afford to make any assumptions. I hurried into the store.

And here she was again. I had promised myself that if I
ever saw her again, I would take a chance. Before I could
think, I crossed over to the other platform. Then, the uptown
express train came. I ran fast, but the train was screeching

out of the station just as I reached the bottom of the stairs. I cursed out loud.

"Missed your ride home?" said a soft, low voice. She was behind me, smiling, her arms crossed under her chest.

She was a little girl, big-eyed and big-mouthed. Her perspiration-matted hair was in a bun. In the V before her coat clasped, I could see her naked, glistening skin. I gawked at her, trying to think of how to start. "You went to a club tonight?" She nodded. It was now or never. "Clit Club?"

"Hell, no," she said, laughing. "Is that where you were?" She eyed me scornfully.

I shook my head. "Where did you go?"

"Nell's."

Time to try again. "Do you know Boy?" Boy was a lesbian bartender there.

"No," she said, brightly. "I only know Jimmy."

I had run out of angles. I stood there feeling foolish, hands in my pockets. She looked away. As loose as her swing coat was, I could see the curve of her bosom. I wanted to undo the coat and see what she was wearing. It couldn't have been much, because her coat wasn't very long and her big, firm legs were in green fishnet stockings.

My train went by. We stood in the near-empty station in silence. Finally, she said, "Since you aren't one for conversation, would you like to read my magazine?" I looked down. She was handing me a copy of "The Advocate." I laughed. "Overgrown as you are and don't know how to take care of business," she pouted.

"I know how to take care of business."

"Yeah?" She looked up, her kohled eyes bright.

I nodded. "Why don't you show me what I'm going to have to work with?" I said, undoing her coat. She was wearing a low, square-necked green dress that revealed the straps of her lacy red bra. I pulled at the neckline. Her breasts were large and soft and the nipples chocolate dark. I put my hand over her crotch. Her thighs were squeezed tightly together. She wasn't wearing any underwear and I could feel her mound.

"It's kind of bushy," she said, shyly.

"I think I can manage," I said, leaning into her. Her smelled of White Linen. Her breasts pressed against my abdomen. She had parted my jacket and was burying her face in my jersey. I ran my hands down and up her back and began to massage her shoulders. I pressed her flesh harder and harder. "You must have an awful lot of tension," I said. She nodded, her cheek rubbing against my breasts. You can always tell how hard a girl can take it by how hard you can massage her shoulders, and she could take it real hard. I pushed her away a little so I could slide my hands into her coat and touch her skin. She tilted her head up, looking at me. I bent down and kissed her soft red lips. She drew my tongue into her mouth with her tongue and began to suck on it. She was reaching up to me, standing on her toes, pressing so hard I had to resist falling backwards. "How have you been left so hungry, a pretty girl like you?" I asked, finally.

"It's a cruel world," she replied. She moved her hands down my front and up the jersey and over my breasts. She began to tease my nipples. Then she tried to lift the jersey up.

"You are getting just little bit wild," I said, pushing it down. She pouted again. Her lips were lusciously thick. "I guess I need to calm you down." She tilted her head, considering the idea. "Are you coming to Brooklyn, or do you have to go home to your lover?"

"You think I'd be this hungry if I had one?" she asked.

I nodded. She laughed. "I haven't been with anyone in a year, which is why I am letting you pick me up. I've given up being good."

"No, you haven't." I kissed the top of her head. "You're real good." And though I was on a tight budget, I knew I couldn't wait. I was going to have to take her somewhere where I could lie her down. Feeling a girl up in the subway station is fine, but this one needed a more activist treatment. My underwear was so moist it was becoming a thong. I told her we were taking a cab.

She nodded. We went up the stairs into the cold night and hailed a taxi. The cabdriver was Indian, and they had a roaring conversation in Hindi as I wiggled my fingers in her fishnet and into her wet hole. Her juices were thick as honey. She reached up and moved closer to the partition and I slid deeper inside her. "Hanh, hanh," she said vigorously to the cabdriver. Finally, we arrived at her apartment. She reached into my pocket and paid the driver. I discreetly wiped my wet fingers on my jeans. "You know how bad I wanted to suck them," I whispered in her ear.

We rushed up the stairs and into her studio. She didn't turn on the lights. I locked the door and she slowly undressed.

I sat on the bed. When she was naked, she came and sat on my lap. I stroked her breasts, and began to lick their tips quickly. She pushed her breast into my mouth. "So suck them," she whispered, her fingers in my dreads and massaging my head. I lay back and pulled her on top of me so her wet crotch was on my stomach. Her heavy breasts caressed my face. I slid my fingers back into her soft, yielding hole. She moaned. She was getting incredibly wet.

"You better undress before I get your clothes dirty," she said, lifting up.

I squeezed her breasts. "Do you have a dildo?"

She jumped up off me. "Didn't you say I'm pretty?" she demanded. I nodded. "Okay, so you are in bed with a pretty girl, and she's naked and she has her legs open to you and all you can come up with is to shove a piece of plastic in her?" She shook her head in dismay.

I laughed. "You can't take anything else."

"Yes, I can." Her voice was like steam. I shook my head, pulling off my clothes. "Yes, I can." She yanked at my jersey. She seized my breasts and began to flick my nipples with her thumbs. "You know you want to," she said, when I was naked, and she pulled my left thigh over hers. Dangling her breasts just out of reach of my mouth, she pressed her pussy against mine and rubbed herself against me, her back arched. I could feel her lips crushed against mine, and I could tell she had a prominent clitoris. I imagined what her pussy looked like but imagining wasn't good enough. I tossed her down.

She opened her thighs, stretching her legs out. Her mound was bisected by a wavy line. I peeled open her labia and her clitoris bulged like a jelly bean. She was wet, but my hand is big, so I asked if she had any KY. She shook her head impatiently and lifted her hips. I told myself to stop because her hole was too tight and she couldn't take it but my fingers plunged into her. I wiggled in my thumb. Her thick, soft, honeyed walls pushed against me but I forged deeper into her, and the walls receded. I curled my fingers into a fist. She pressed her thighs together and turned to her side.

"Is it too much?" I asked, my other hand reaching for myself.

In response, she turned onto her stomach with one leg raised so I could move more deeply inside her. I pushed and

TRUE STORY

pulled my hand inside her as she moved her ass back and forth. She mewled as I plunged until I hit her plug, and her canal was flooded. She raised onto all fours and I began to fist her more rapidly, jamming into her until she was so open that I could pull out completely and easily move back in. Her thick cream poured onto my hand, arm, even elbow. She screamed. "Don't hurt me," she gasped.

I stopped. "Do you want me to pull out?" She shook her head. "You don't know how much you can take," I said, sitting back on my feet.

She looked at me over her shoulder. Huskily she said, "Make me come."

I reached around her waist to fondle her breasts. "Baby, I knew it would be too much for you." I kissed her back. She rested her head on the pillow, raised her ass and purred insistently. I ran my tongue down her spine. My hand was still inside her and I knew it would hurt her if I pulled out now. It would be much easier on her if I did it as she came. I moved inside her. She made low, quick noises.

I sped up. Her pussy was getting hotter and her softness was pushing against my fist as I shoved into her. It felt so good as her pussy responded to me, her meat sucking me in and trying to eject me out. My arm began to ache but I couldn't stop. My crotch was tingling. I squeezed my muscles and fisted her fast. She rocked and moaned, louder and louder until she sprayed out come like hot oil over my chest. Quickly, I pulled out. I licked her salty sauce off my fingers.

She turned on her back and I lay over her. She ran her fingers lightly over my skin. We kissed slowly and lazily, until my pussy couldn't wait any longer. "Come on, baby," I said, pulling her on top of me.

"Why should I?" she sulked. I was aghast. "You made me wait."

"When did I make you wait?" I began rubbing myself.

"You didn't see me on Hudson Street a couple of months ago?" she said, her eyes half-closed, her sweet, thick lower lip quivering. "You made me wait until now to take care of business."

"I'm sorry, baby," I said, over and over again, barely coherently. I was in agony. The sight of her hole so open to my fist had made my pussy extraordinarily greedy. "Please."

"Why don't you wait a few months?" she said. I shifted around uncomfortably. My own hand was not enough. "Didn't your mother ever tell you not to torture little girls?" she said, kissing my abdomen. I grabbed her by her hair. She eyed me defiantly. "Say you'll never make me wait again."

"Never," I said and shoved her head between my legs. She opened my pussy and ran her tongue over it lightly, too lightly do anything but torture me. Then, she laughed and began to suck my pussy, first gently, then harder. She nibbled delicately at my lips, then licked my clitoris rapidly. I pulled hard on her breasts until she sucked me again. She ran her tongue in the grooves between my folds until she reached the centre and firmly picked up my clitoris by the stem with her mouth and sucked me until I came in waves. She opened my thighs further and shoved her breasts against my throbbing cunt.

Finally, I pulled her up onto me. Her small body was heavy and warm and soft. I pulled the covers over us. "Don't forget," she said, sleepily. "Don't make me have to really punish you."

I laughed. "I won't forget, baby," I said. And you know, I never did.

Jess Wells

Journeys of an Ancient Lady

Muriel stood on the train platform, staring at the rippled sides of the oily train as if into the face of a loved one. Her gray suit, nearly the colour of the train, was rumpled despite her efforts to remain crisp and tailored when she travelled. At sixty-five, her hair was now snowy white, without a trace of the red that had been her trademark for so many years. It still wisped around her face, unruly, evidence that she refused, unlike so many women her age, to pin and tuck, spray, curl or net. It was over now, her incredible journey, a lifetime of travel, and the sensations ran over her skin: the smell of warm arms, the press of lips against her thighs, the aroma of wet hair, the touch of silk and burlap, of cotton sheets still hanging on the line as her body was pressed into them. Whose breath was it that she could feel against the soft skin between her lip and nose? All of them, all the lovers who let slip the acrid smell of calamari, the sweet of Schnapps on clean teeth, the musk of wine and nutty tobacco, all sighing against her face, their tiny breaths full of gratitude and self-absorption.

She swayed unsteadily as the train wrenched itself from the platform, gathering speed, tearing her past away from her and leaving her coated with a cindery dust and the stench of diesel. She took a step backward as her knees buckled and she fell into a faint on her luggage.

"Telegram for Muriel Fitzwater!" the thin voice of the young boy had pronounced at the desk of the college dormitory more than 40 years ago.

"Come at once Andover House. Nanna dying. No refusal allowed," the telegram said. Muriel pushed her bright red hair from her face and exchanged her room key for an envelope of dismissal papers, strode into the New England sunlight and hailed a cab.

Muriel slipped into the dark where Nanna's companion sat near the bed holding the old woman's hand. Surrounded by her grandmother's lace and tapestries, china on pedestals, Moroccan leather boxes, Asian masks, and glistening Italian marble eggs, Muriel looked out of place. She tried to straighten her rough cotton shirt and thread-worn Chinos. She laid her brown leather jacket on a tufted chair and approached the bed. Her grandmother opened her eyes and smiled.

"And a red head, no less," Nanna muttered, then began to laugh, closing her eyes. "Another goddamn red head."

Tricksey smiled with bright healthy teeth and gray eyes.

"Gretchen has a task for you," Tricksey said gravely to Muriel. Tricksey, who reminded Muriel of a sparrow, retrieved a small yellow envelope and handed it to Gretchen.

The old woman tried to raise herself onto the pillows.

"This is a list," her grandmother said. "You must go to

every one of these people, in the order in which their names are written on the pieces of paper and tell them," the woman said, stopping for breath, closing her eyes, then looking directly into Muriel's eyes, "tell them I have...always loved them."

"Don't try to skip anyone," Tricksey warned, "we'll know if you do."

"When you return, Tricksey will give you..."

"Perhaps we should wait, Gretchen. Wait for her to return from the first leg of her journey," Tricksey said, picking up Gretchen's hand.

"No, no," Gretchen said, closing her eyes and falling asleep. Muriel stepped forward and grasped the bedstead. Her grandmother, nearly a stranger to her, looked very much like the photos her mother had kept on the mantle. The photos showed a beautiful woman, with soft skin and high cheekbones. Now aged, her grandmother was very pale but seemed to radiate, even from her deathbed, and Muriel looked at her curiously, as if her grandmother wasn't dying from sickness but was somehow melting, like fine china tossed into fire. Tricksey watched the woman sleep, not moving her palms from around Gretchen's thin, veined hand.

Gretchen woke and sighed.

"You will give her..." Tricksey prompted.

"Tricksey will give you one hundred thousand dollars when we have evidence that your chore has been completed. Do you understand?"

"One hundred thousand...," Muriel said, astounded.

"That's right, dear," Tricksey said. "Of course one hundred thousand would be just an installment toward the total."

"Go ahead and tell her," Gretchen murmured.

"There is thirteen million dollars to be distributed if you agree to take part in our little...project, shall we say."

"You want me to...convey your love?" Muriel said sceptically, trying to cover her astonishment at the idea of getting her hands on thirteen million dollars. "Nanna, do you want me to write to them?"

"No, no," the old woman said hastily. "These are matters of the flesh, my dear. Paper and ink are not suitable for the conveyance. You must visit each one of them personally, do you understand? Afterward, take the paper their name is written on, and mail it back to us, each in separate envelopes. Proceed to the next piece of paper. Don't get them out of order. Tricksey receives the balance of my estate...and since your parents are no longer with us I don't expect any squabbles," she said. "Will you do this for me?"

"Of course," Muriel said, "but what if I'm gone...for weeks?"

Gretchen laughed and tiredly closed her eyes. "I expect you shall be, my dear. I certainly expect you shall."

"I love you, Nanna," Muriel said softly. The scent of old-fashioned laundry soap rose from the sheets as she bent and pressed her lips into the woman's soft cheek.

"You must leave immediately," the woman said. "The rest of this is not for you."

Muriel gripped the bed covers, as her grandmother, smiling weakly, slowly raised a hand and stroked her cheek. "You're a dear one."

Tricksey escorted Muriel into the hall and poured a cup of tea as Muriel nervously paced pack and forth, her jacket slung over the sagging shoulders of her white cotton shirt.

"I should have visited more often," Muriel said, taking the cup and looking away.

"Nonsense," Tricksey said compassionately. "She only

just arrived home a few years ago. She wasn't much of a grandmother to you, but...she will be. Here's a portion of the first allotment for expenses. More will be sent to your destinations. Now go," she said, taking the tea cup from Muriel's hand and escorting her to the door.

"Tricksey, my darling," the old woman called from the next room. "Come and dance with me again," Gretchen implored softly. Tricksey smiled and opened the door wider for Muriel's departure.

"In a heartbeat, my dearest," she called.

As the tram sped across the crowded streets of Stockholm, Muriel fingered the small envelope, a map and a phrase book. A hundred thousand dollars, and an all-expenses-paid trip through Europe. She could do worse for a graduation gift. She hadn't known her grandmother was that rich. Sure, her grandmother had been paying for that girlie school all these years, ivy up the ass and women who still said things like "lavaliered." But filthy rich, that was something else.

"Jana Stor, at 652 Trootim Street," Muriel recited to herself. Perhaps a cup of tea, then on to the Youth Hostel. Nothing complicated. The woman was even in the phone book. Perhaps this would not be a bad way to earn money, she thought to herself as the tram slowed, then jolted to a stop.

"Pardon me, madam," she said to the maid who answered the door and motioned her into the hall. "Gretchen Fitzwater has sent me —"

"Fitzwater?" the maid interrupted.

"Yes. My grandmother Gretchen Fitzwater, has requested that I —"

"Just a moment please." The maid allowed her to step

into the hallway, then turned and hurried through a large ornate living room. Rather confused, Muriel shifted the rucksack on her shoulder. She heard a large door open and close quietly behind the maid, then open again almost immediately.

"You may see Madam Stor," the maid said. "This way." Muriel ran her hand through her hair and attempted to straighten her white cotton shirt. At the large wooden door to the library, the maid reached out her hand for Muriel's rucksack and after Muriel entered, closed the door behind her.

Muriel cleared her throat, looked around at the high-ceilings, the white sunshine that bathed the muslin curtains and the pale flowered upholstery.

"So, you've come on Gretchen's behalf," a husky voice said.

Muriel turned, suddenly seeing a woman in the corner, standing behind an expansive desk that was draped in a rust-coloured cloth. The dramatic pattern of the cloth and the riotous leaves of a potted plant behind her nearly obscured the outline of the woman.

"Yes. I'm sorry to just appear on your doorstep, but —"

"But that's the way Gretchen set it up. I know, I know," the woman said, stepping towards Muriel. She was tall and broad shouldered, with white hair pinned into a french twist. As she walked toward Muriel, her clothing, yards of gold and brown and rust hanging from her shoulders, rippled with her movement. The woman shook her hand, then cupped Muriel's face. Muriel swallowed hard. The woman's blue eyes were like ice chips.

"Did you know your grandmother?" the woman asked, still holding her face very close to her own.

"No. I'm afraid I...didn't," Muriel said, thinking how

she didn't call, didn't visit, never stayed long during holidays even though her grandmother was the closest living relative after her parents died.

"That's a pity," the woman said, turning and motioning towards a large sofa. "So," the woman said softly as she sat, "I suppose this means she's dying."

"Yes," Muriel breathed, hesitantly lowering her long frame onto the couch. "Did you know about...my arrival? Did Nanna plan this?"

"No, no," the woman said, unconvincingly. "I had no idea she was dying. My God, we're going to miss her."

"I don't know if this is the proper moment, so forgive me if I'm being inappropriate." As the words came off her tongue, Muriel was suddenly flooded with the understanding that Jana indeed, had been loved and cherished by many, and had filled her ample, supple flesh with the emotions and devotions of others. Muriel could see Jana sitting with her robe open in the morning, savouring biscuits and last night's activities. "She's sent me to tell you...," Muriel explained softly, then looked around the room to be sure they were alone, "that...she's always loved you."

The woman looked away, touched the tips of her teeth with her tongue. "Then she is dying. And she's sent you," the woman said, smiling sadly. She touched Muriel's cheek with the palm of her hand, pushed her hair behind her ear. "You will stay with me awhile, won't you?" the woman said, very softly, sitting far too close to Muriel.

"Well, I have...um," Muriel thought, hesitant to tell the woman that she suspected she had a number of women to visit, though she didn't know who or where. Muriel couldn't quite decide if these women had been friends or lovers of her grandmother. Either way, no one likes to think of themselves as just a name on a list.

"Yes, yes, but you will stay. Won't you?"

"I could, for a short time," Muriel said hesitantly. "That's very generous of you. Thank you."

"And the sauna, you're fond of the sauna?"

"Yes," Muriel said. "It was quite a flight."

"I'll have a car brought around."

The Central Stockholm Sauna was enormous, the size of discos in New York. Muriel stripped off her clothing in front of the lockers on the second-floor balcony. The balcony was a complex of lockers and wooden benches, where women slowly wove in and out, stripping off panties, twisting thick terry-cloth around their waists.

Muriel was nearly six-feet tall, sizable even among these Swedes. She had a taut belly and muscled thighs, and small, firm breasts. Her gray eyes were reassuring after one was startled by her wild red hair. Her underarm hair was thick and auburn, on her legs the hair was fine and carrot-like. She threw a towel over her shoulder, tossed her clothing into a locker, and headed for the stairs. A sauna, an envelope, a bit of dinner and, in the morning, off to the next name.

The steam mixed with the sweat and the smell of herbs rising from women's skin as it rose from the pool, up the blue, chipped tile of the main wall. Water poured from a fountain. Muriel slowly descended into the water. Its heat shocked her skin but she kept moving toward the deep end until she was swimming toward the far corner, where Jana was approaching.

Jana's translucent white skin, tight over her legs and hipbones, was soft and yielding over her belly. Her white hair hung like a veil down her back which was slightly stooped now that she was relieved of her proper library and big house. Muriel was still in the water. Jana had voluminous breasts, full and vibrant as she stepped down the stairs, carefully, gracefully. She cradled her heavy, precious breasts in her arms as if carrying an armload of fruit. Muriel looked at them with awe and watched Jana slide into the water, her succulent breasts rising to chest level and freeing her hands to stroke through the blue water. Muriel swam to her, pulled towards the buttery skin. She leaned against the smooth tile wall, the fountain pounding water inches from her shoulder. Jana moved in front of her, reached out and cupped Muriel's wet head in her hand, drew herself near.

"You'll stay with me in my time of grief, won't you?" Jana whispered at Muriel's lips. Muriel's breath came short and fast as Jana pressed her breasts into Muriel and held her close.

Weeks of sliding her lips along the warmth of Jana's breasts became months of grasping the softness of the woman's ass. She laid under Jana's quilts for six months, watched every morning as the woman brushed and twisted her incredible length of silver hair, and each time the mane flipped over in Jana's hands, Muriel relived the feeling of it slapping against her body. She could have eaten more herring, sipped more gin and taken a year's worth of walks along the water's edge on the woman's arm, but yesterday when she had gone to the *poste restante*, there was no envelope with another check, just an envelope with a name. It was time to go, she thought reluctantly. When Muriel walked out the front door for the last time, she felt so surrounded by Jana's flesh, so broken down and defenceless by the melted quality of Jana's body, that she felt it nearly unsafe to be in the world of strangers.

Envelope to envelope, Muriel pursued her task. Seven countries, seven lovers. Muriel leaned her head against the starched linen headrest on the train seat and closed her eyes.

She had been having so much sex that the movement of the train became her back rocking under mosquito netting. Her arm dropping off the seat was the languishing gesture of the moment she gave in to being laid across a table. The train coursing around a corner was the time a lover had spun her through Mediterranean water until the sea and sky had only her naked body between them. She walked through the women's houses with an eye to each woman in the room: Who will be my lover now? she wondered at her destinations. She became aroused each time she raised her hand to knock on another door.

Yet, shouldn't she have plans of her own? she wondered, deliriously. With a degree in Medieval Culture, what were her choices? Work as a clerk for twelve dollars an hour if she were lucky, or make love around the world for more money than she could spend in a lifetime? Seemed a very clear-cut choice, but not one that could stop the uneasy questions in her sleep. She had lost a sense of where she was going or why, moving without a destination that was not completely chartered by manila envelopes pressed inside her passport. Without strife for money or self-determination, it seemed her life had no meaning except as a journey towards the flames of another lover.

In Barcelona, the long boulevard smelled of chestnuts as Muriel flopped onto a bench, exasperated. She had been winding through the narrow, cobbled streets, crossing the *Ramblas* with its gnarled leafless trees and newspaper stands, following what she thought was the route to the *Calle de Cabarello*, only to discover she was following the smell of fried squid. Cabs did not run through the Gothic Quarter so there was no way to simply put herself in someone else's hands and every time she asked directions she was sent on a twisted course that was different from the last directions she had gotten. She had looked all day yesterday to no avail and today it seemed she would fail as well.

She turned into a market, the tin roof reverberating with the shouts of women calling for a kilo of oranges, a better price for chicken. Muriel proffered her slip of paper, embarrassed that all she could utter was a rude *"Donde es?"* into the women's harried and sweating faces. They pinched the note between their oil-stained fingers, then waved her on. Finally, a woman behind a stall of pistachios grabbed her by the wrist.

"Gabriella!" she shouted, then tossed Muriel's wrist away and talked with a woman in a shapeless black dress and shawl. Muriel cleared her throat and bowed her head nervously as the woman looked up at Muriel's red hair and raised her eyebrows. Did the woman know her purpose? Muriel attempted a shy smile. The black-garbed woman disappeared into the crowd. Muriel quickly followed behind her as she walked through a labyrinth of narrow streets, with darkened, shuttered old buildings dotted by heavy wooden doors.

The woman in black opened a small door that was set into a large pair of oak doors studded with black iron hinges and pegs. Muriel bent to enter and stood in a courtyard with old vegetation in large clay pots. The woman motioned her to a bench, upon which Muriel sat with her rucksack in her lap. She watched a large fountain in the middle of the courtyard. Suddenly, a young woman in a mint-green sundress grabbed Muriel's hand, pulled her into a room that was down a corridor off the courtyard and shut the door.

The woman stood three feet in front of her, her eyes bright and her full lips pressed against laughter that tensed her jaw. Her inch long hair lay like fine silk on her scalp. She was as thin as a reed with huge dark eyes. She clapped her hands together and laughed. Muriel smiled at her, embarrassed.

"Gretchen Fitzwater...," she began, but the woman opened her hands, laughed again and pressed her palms together.

"Yes, yes," the woman said with a thick Spanish accent.

Muriel pushed back her curly red hair. The woman giggled, then filled the quiet room with peals of laughter.

"I saw you there," the woman said, "I thought — so serious! This woman needs some fun. Plenty of time for my grandmama, yes?"

"Yes," Muriel said emphatically. She could ignore the list for a moment. Make a friend of her own. Someone her age.

The woman smiled and reached for a white shawl that hung on a peg. The scent of her perfume warmed Muriel's nostrils.

The woman, Anya, took her to cafés where the squid was pulled steaming of sea and garlic from ovens in the stone walls, then to bars where they held double-spouted decanters into the air as they poured its red wine down their throats. They ate pastries at street-side canteenas made of old gypsy wagons, holding hands under the chest-high counter. At dawn, they were the first to nestle into chairs at the long marble tables of a café where hundreds of canaries chirped from cages on the walls.

Exhausted, they crept into the back door of Anya's house and into her bed, where Muriel kissed the down on her belly and the crest of her hipbones as if Anya had saved her, released her from her state of servitude. She burned the taste of the woman's sex into her mind as something precious and private. This was not a woman on the list, not a woman her grandmother had ever known. Maybe Muriel finally was living her own life, regardless of the money. She grasped Anya's ankles and ran her hands fiercely up her legs, trying to remember, to prove something to herself. After Anya had climaxed, arching her back off the sheets and digging her nails into the bedposts, it was Muriel's tears that collected in a puddle in the soft dip of Anya's collarbone.

It was nearly noon when Anya put Muriel into her white shirt and the khaki pants that were crumpled from the journey and, with a firm hand on her back, pushed her out the back door.

"You are expected now," Anya whispered as Muriel reluctantly headed out the door.

Anya's grandmother greeted Muriel in the courtyard, ordered that tea and bread be brought to a long iron table under the largest tree. Entirely swathed in brown, the old woman's tiny veined hands and small lined face peeked from the dress, shawl and brown lace mantilla that cascaded onto the courtyard tiles. She asked Muriel to pass a plate of pastries that were sitting within the woman's grasp. Her eyes were unchanging as Muriel rose, came to her end of the table, and lifted the plate to a spot inches from her face.

"Where are the pastries?" the woman said.

Muriel bent forward slightly, leaned from side to side and then realized the woman was blind.

"Oh," Muriel said, setting the plate of pastries into the woman's hands. "I'm very sorry."

"I don't see well any more," the old woman said. "Anya insists that I tell people but it is one of last vanities I have. That and," she said, removing the mantle of lace, "dying my hair. Is it lovely?"

"Yes," Muriel said, surprised at the lustrous brown mane of hair, nearly the colour of her dress, that curled from her crown to her shoulders.

Muriel's eye was caught by a movement upstairs on the balcony above the courtyard. At first she thought it was curtains blowing in the breeze but she then caught a glimpse of Anya. She wore a short vest that barely covered her small, tight breasts, bare thighs and brown ass as she moved languidly from room to room. Muriel instinctively looked back at the grandmother to see if the woman had noticed her longing gaze, then slyly looked up at the balcony again. Anya had walked outside and was now leaning on the wrought-iron railing. She cupped her breasts, the black vest gathering under her soft arms. She turned her head from side to side as she kneaded her breasts and squeezed her nipples. Muriel gripped her tea cup. Anya closed her eyes and tightly gripped her nipples. She slung her leg around a wrought-iron pole and pressed her breasts against either side of the cool metal. Anya moved across the balcony and slipped into another room. Muriel picked up the plate of pastries. "Pastry?" she said.

"*Si, por favor*, one with jam."

"Madam," Muriel said, wishing to fulfil her task, as she retook her seat, "my grandmother has sent me —"

The old woman held up her thin hand.

"That is a conversation for sherry and fruit," the woman said. "Anya!" she called in a reed-like voice. Still in her vest, her triangle of black hair gleaming in the sun, her olive skin radiant, the girl slowly descended the courtyard stairs.

"*Si*, grandma. Time for a delicious meal, yes? The maid is gone. I will fix you your favourite," she said, not taking her eyes off Muriel.

"Oh, yes," the woman shrieked with delight. "Our guest must certainly be one for a feast. I used to lament my failing eyesight," the woman said as Anya retreated into the kitchen, "but it just makes more wonderful the taste of things, the smell."

"Yes," Muriel said, her skin prickling with the danger of Anya's nakedness and her own part in the charade. "Madam, I have been sent —"

"I won't hear a word of it," the woman said sternly. "You must enjoy your dinner. Then you may deliver your message. Allow an old woman to control what little she can."

Anya had slipped a knee-length apron over her vest, leaving it untied so it swung over each of her hips, exposing her muff as she walked. She delivered a bounty of food while facing her grandmother, leaning far over the table at Muriel's elbow until her body lay nearly horizontal along its length. Her tight buttocks greeted Muriel as Anya set down bowls of wrinkled black olives, heads of garlic fried in olive oil, moist red pimentos striped black from the searing pan. Muriel's mouth opened, instinctively. Anya continued until the table was nearly covered with pungent, steaming foodstuffs barely contained in their plates and bowls. Her grandmother, without seeing the contents, brought each to her face, groped for the spoon wedged among the morsels and filled her plate, smiling. Muriel ladled food onto her plate, then reached for eggplant dotted with sun-dried tomatoes. She gasped. Hands gripped her ankles, moved quickly up to her thighs. Anya had slipped under the table, and was grasping the edge of Muriel's panties. Pushing her fingers into Muriel's ass, Anya stripped them off and lay her warm lips on Muriel's thighs.

"You must have some of the olives," the grandmother said as a shiver ran along Muriel's spine.

"It's delicious," Muriel said nervously and picked up her fork. She brought the eggplant to her lips, and Anya brought her lips to Muriel. In Muriel's mouth, the taste of the rich food mingled with the heat rising through her body and the texture of the pungent dinner with the feel of Anya's tongue. She struggled to breathe into her excitement and spoon food into her mouth. She bit into her fork, gripped her wine glass.

Each time she stopped for breath, to drop her fork and seize the edge of her chair, Anya stopped.

"Eat your dinner," the old woman admonished. "I can't hear you eating." Muriel panted, looked over the table to see what delight she hadn't savoured. She carefully lifted herself from her chair, leaning over the table to reach a plate. Anya thrust her fingers deep inside Muriel who collapsed back into her chair, fighting the pounding desire to let out a moan that would make the birds fly out of the tree above them.

"Yes, of course you enjoy my beautiful meal," the old woman said.

Muriel slunk lower into her chair, slipping a bit of fruit compote into her mouth, gliding it along her teeth as Anya dug her fingers deeper inside and again lowered her lips to Muriel's sex.

"And now," the old woman said, "I'll leave you girls to your desert." Muriel's eyes widened. She blushed wildly, her mouth dropped open and her vulva clutched at Anya's presence. The old woman rose, and groping for the edge of the table to get her bearings, stepped with great caution toward the open door to the library.

Muriel and Anya joined the old woman later. She was standing at the mantle of a huge fireplace, fingering the ornate silver frames of old photographs.

"I'd like to deliver a message from my grandmother," Muriel said firmly.

"Grandma," Anya said, "Muriel has decided to abandon

her quest. She's returning home, without her mission fulfilled."

The old woman was very quiet, then turned, still clutching a frame.

"There are some women born into the world for small passions," the woman said. "They marry. They dig and scratch for small bits of love." She ran her hand along the edges of a frame. "A dog perhaps. A rose bush. If they are lucky, a daughter. But women like you, my dear, are born for big love," she said, fiercely pulling the frame to her chest. "Love like that gives the world it's humid smell," she laughed. "It is your duty to sweat into the rivers, little Muriel, to be fire on a hillside. Live it, grasp it in both hands and hold it tight against your lips. Do it for the rest of us. Poor, pitiful things, we scramble for love that is no deeper than...the lick of a selfish cat. Continue your journey for those of us who can only stay at home and dream of your adventures."

Muriel stood very quietly for a moment, then walked to the old woman, and kissed her on her soft lips.

"She always...loved you," Muriel said tenderly. She returned to Anya's side, grasping her soft shoulders.

"Come with me," she whispered.

Anya gestured to her grandmother and shook her head.

Muriel pressed her cheek against Anya's in pain, stepped away, and headed towards the train.

When Muriel awoke, forty years later, she gazed up at the soft white linen of her grandmother's canopy bed, her own snowy hair fanned out on the pillow.

"Tricksey?" she said sleepily.

"No, I'm her successor, so to speak. Only just returned a year ago. And the marvelous news is, I think we've found someone in your lineage to carry on your task. Care to begin a list for her, my dear?"

"Another list?"

"As I understand it, your lovers only. That is, no one from the previous list."

Muriel smiled. She laughed the tired, sweet laughter of a woman seeing the beauty of a grand design. In a soft wool suit and gold jewellery, Tricksey's replacement sat with a smile, pen in hand.

"We have to leave our money to someone, darling," she said.

"Anya de Jesus," Muriel said dreamily. "Penny White-water. Maria Ricci. Suzanna Fujimoto..."

BETH BRANT

So Generously

Even now, the texture of your voice over the phone covers me with memory of your silk-brown skin, your nipples brushing my own, your tongue marking trails on my neck, my mouth, my shoulders.

Your breath in my ear — "Te amo." The sound of your voice this night has carried me to the place of writing.

I told you then I would write poems to you.
Years later, I am writing this one.

Something I could give you — years after our heated, rushed love, spanning only thirty days — the residue of those nights and days remains inside me like the scent from the passion-soaked sheets lingered in your room.
I spread my legs and my body to you. I spread my self to you, opening and opening to every touch and word you caressed on me.

"Te amo," you whispered. "Mi corazon," you sang.

Your fingers on my back as we danced, the brush of your hand on my arm as we rode the subway, the way you held a book, the way you moved, the way you talked, the colour of your eyes — like black stones found in the sea; wet, beautiful, full of story. All these made heat rise in me.

Hot for you, wet for you.
My wetness; flowing, waiting to coat your fingers and hands, your lips and tongue.
Hot for you. Wet for you.
Kissing me as you rose from my open thighs, I would taste the liquid of myself on your tongue.

You made tapes of Willie Colon, Luciecita, Armando Reyes — knowing I would never listen to this music again without remembering the humidity of your room — candles lit, flowers placed in front of the image of La Virgen, bowls of water and salt flanking her picture. The dish of sand from your beloved Puerto Rico, the rosary of your mother laid across the white cloth. Each day you placed bread upon this altar.
I watched your hands perform this act of love, then turned to receive your body in another act of love.

You asked me to run away with you to your island. I imagined your land as you wove the descriptions to me. I could smell the water surrounding your land as I touched your breasts. I could taste the fruits of your land as I put my fingers inside you, then licked the cream that poured from you.

I knew I would not run with you, but I imagined your island.
And told you I would write poems to you.

Poems that would detail our meeting:
"I only fall for women who have Scorpio rising," you joked.
"I have Scorpio rising," I said.
Your confident, loud laughter as you took my hand and kissed my life-line.
"Somehow, I knew that," and your lips burned the lines that mapped across my palm.

Poems that would describe the Staten Island ferry, the restaurants we ate in, the New York stories, your neighbourhood of pimps and junkies tangled with new yuppies who came to exorcise the streets.

Poems about the presents you gave me — the topaz earrings, the flowers, the ring from Guatemala, the Tarot cards, the silk blouse you bought because it was the colour of my eyes.
"A blue-eyed Indian," you sighed as you kissed my eyelids.
"Tell me about this blue-eyed Indian." And I told you secrets about myself. Secrets I knew would be guarded by you.

Poems about the food you cooked for me. The sauce of garlic and oil that coated the platanos, yami and chocho with an opaque sheen. The carne stews, the rice, the thick, black coffee you boiled on the stove, adding sugar and milk until it became a confection.

Poems about your political activism for Puerto Rican independence, your marxist-feminist analysis of everything, the gentleness towards your sisters who were locked in prison and whom you visited as often as possible; carrying sweets and flowers that were inevitably confiscated, but you persevered and fought for the right of beauty in that ugly world.

Poems that were scented with the sweat underneath your large breasts, the liquid between your legs, the black curling hair of your cunt, the dark mauve of your clitoris before you came, the salty-sweetness of your back.

Poems about your tenderness and roughness, the glorious revelling in our sex, the love words, the sex words whispered between us — Spanish and English mingling like our smells — lush vapour, close in your magic room.
"Say it, say it," you whispered between my legs.
And I would speak with waves upon waves of orgasm, my body shaking and soaring into a land of tropical heat and dust-covered roads, canopies of trees, sounds of ocean lapping against sand.

I was going to write poems to you.
Years later there is this.

Each day was going to be my last with you.
Your voice, heavy with sex, "Te amo," and I would postpone the journey home.
I had come here when the air was still cold, snow falling outside Gloria's apartment, and too soon the trees in Central Park began leafing new green, the whores on Alphabet Street were shedding coats to better display their skinny bodies to customers, the junkies were nodding off in the sun.

It was not my intention to give anything up, especially myself.

Nor did I.

I had no intentions, no plans, no wishes.

Your call was fierce, sweet, and my answer mirrored your fierceness, matched your sweetness.

Our last night, the candles burning a hot, steady flame, you again touched every part of me that could bring pleasure. You held my face in your hands and licked the tears — a mixture of yours and mine.

"Women leave me. Why?"

Now, as we talk on the phone from time to time, your voice raised in outrage at the latest political atrocity, the latest homophobic attack, you recite the latest failed relationship — married women, straight women, unfaithful women.

Exasperated, I say that you only find what you are looking for, women who will always leave you.

"You don't want a solid relationship," I say, "only ones that will prove your ability to make a conquest."

"Si, querida," you say. "So, when are you coming to New York again?"

You laugh, and in my mind's eye, I see your full, dark lips drawn across your white even teeth, and I want to feel those lips on mine and on my body, sucking my breasts, sucking out the honeyed liquid that flows so readily at the sound of your voice.

I laugh with you.

"I have never made love with a grandmother," you say teasingly.

"You must be losing your touch."

"I haven't lost my touch, mi corazon. Perhaps you have just forgotten it."

I have not forgotten your touch. It comes to me at times I least expect — a gift from the conscious past — wrapped in brown silk and carrying the smell of botanicas where we purchased candles and magic herbs. I have not forgotten your touch.

We have seen each other through the years — at conferences, at seminars. I am always careful to not be alone with you, except in the safe places of cafes. You send me birthday cards and presents each May. We talk on the phone, your calls taking place during the day when you know I will be alone.

I keep your letters and cards in a special place, alongside the topaz earrings, the take-out menu from Ming Gardens, the dried roses from the bouquet you gave me at the airport on our last day in New York.

But even in the safety of cafes, your gestures and voice bring back memory of wet nights, wet bodies, wet places of love. The smell of you as you laboured to bring forth every sensation from my being. Reaching into my body for response, your hands entering all parts of me and your whispers of "Te amo, te amo. Speak to me, querida. Say it, say it."

I spoke in the language of my body.
The speech of my willing skin.
The dialect of my swollen nipples.
The accent of breath upon soft thighs.
The phrases of shouts and sighs of joy and release.

Years later, I give this poem to you.
It is small next to your abundance of spirit.
So generously you loved me.

I give this to you.
And you will know, querida, this is yet another way to say,
"Te amo."

LUCY JANE BLEDSOE

The Old-Fashioned Way

When I got home, my roommate Erika was hard at work at her typewriter. She sure put in the hours on her writing, I had to give her that.

Erika is a twenty-three-year-old sex radical. She is multiply-pierced and hates anything associated with seventies feminism, including Frye boots and flannel shirts. Her favourite phrase is "sex positive."

"How's the single gal," she asked, ogling me with great exaggeration.

I laughed. At least she had a sense of humour. "Lonely," I said.

She raised an eyebrow. "Miss Nancy?"

"Yeah." I missed her a lot.

"I know a good way to relieve loneliness."

"Erika, honey, are you trying — again — to seduce me?"

"I'm not shy."

"I know. But you're young enough to be my daughter."

"Ha! If you gave birth at thirteen."

"Happens every day."

"I could teach you a few tricks that might come in handy as you start dating again."

"You're that skilled?"

She looked down at the keys of her typewriter, tapped one a couple times. "I've been around."

"Whose bed?"

Her head jerked up. "What?"

"Whose bed? Yours or mine? Or would you rather use the stove top? Burners on or off?"

I wished I could have preserved the look on her face just then. A mix of fear and incredulity. That look made me sincere about wanting to go to bed with her. Under all that sex radical paraphernalia, Erika was a real sweetheart.

She pulled her image together quickly and responded, "I have some great toys in my room."

I hesitated, then said, "Okay." It felt as if a coach was about to introduce me to the equipment in a new gym.

"Now?" she asked.

"I might lose my nerve later," I said, playing up to her show of sophistication.

She smiled indulgently. "It won't hurt a bit," she teased. "Come on." She led me by the hand to her bedroom.

"One rule," I warned.

"What?" She adjusted her face so that it was open, accepting.

"No gerbils."

"Get out of here," she said, pushing me onto her bed.

She stood looking down at me and I laughed. I said, "I don't know if I can kiss my roommate, you know?"

"Who said anything about kissing?"

I laid back. Okay, this twenty-three-year-old kid wanted to run the show. Fine. I was tired.

Erika stripped off her oversized jeans and lumberjack shirt. She wore no bra or underpants. I saw a bit of silver glinting in her pubic hair. I winced at the thought of her pierced clit. What if I snagged the ring and tore it off or something?

I didn't make any moves to take off my own clothes. This was Erika's show. She sat on the bed and ran a hand from my throat down to my belly. I wished the touch had given me some kind of buzz, but it hadn't. She unbuttoned my shirt quickly and pulled it off my shoulders, then unzipped my jeans but left them on me.

Next Erika opened a drawer by her bed and started pulling out toys. I closed my eyes and listened to the appliances clank as she tossed them on the bed. Please don't tie me up, I thought. I really didn't want to be tied up. What was wrong with good old-fashioned sex? Did it really take her a cabinet full of high-tech appliances to get off?

"Can I undress?" I finally asked.

"Sure." Erika stood back to watch. I undid my black lace bra and dropped it to the floor. Erika swallowed. I raised my hips to pull my jeans off my butt. My panties came with them. Then I posed for her, propping myself up on one elbow, extending one leg straight out and crooking the other leg up so that my vulva opened.

"You're beautiful," she said, her voice croaking. For the first time, she didn't sound as if she were speaking from a script.

"When are you gonna stop readying your tools and get to work on me?"

She swallowed again. "Close your eyes," she said, so I did. She sounded like she was saddling up a horse. Finally she said, "Okay."

I opened my eyes. First I looked into Erika's eyes which

were hot green and defiant. She held her mouth, with its very full and very red lips, in a snarl position. Her hands were planted firmly on her narrow hips. "My god!" I shrieked, bucking straight up on the bed, "that's a whale sticking out of your pussy!"

"That's right. I'm gonna shove this whale up —"

"Oh no you're not," I interrupted quickly. "A lavender whale up my vagina is not my idea of —"

"Loosen up, Liz," Erika said, climbing onto the bed with me.

"E-li-za-beth," I said, feeling very tired. "My name is four syllables long."

"To me you're just my whore, my sexy, trashy little whore."

I moaned with disgust, but Erika took it as pleasure. "Oh, yeah," she went on in a growly voice which was entirely different from her regular high voice. "You're a cheap piece of meat to me." She placed her red mouth on my neck like a sea anemone.

"Wait a second," I said, utterly unmoved by her attempts at talking dirty. "Could we just, you know, touch a little first."

"Relax," she said. "Just let your mind go. Your generation spent so much energy taking back the night, you gave up your own pleasure. Try imagining I've just paid three hundred dollars for your gorgeous body. You could get that much, you know."

I laid back, too polite to tell her that I had no problem with talking dirty. I longed for Nancy's trashy mouth. But it's gotta come from the heart. Dirty talk had to come from real passion.

Erika reached under the bed and produced some wrist restraints. She kept trying to talk dirty but sounded more like she'd memorized a bad porn script. I let her tie me to the bed. I let her climb on me, twist my nipples a couple times, then push that lavender whale up me. She pumped away on the dildo muttering, "I'm deep in your ocean, baby." I bucked my hips for her, but I wasn't going to go so far as to fake an orgasm. She didn't come either.

We laid there for a while and didn't talk. I was still tied to the bedposts. The lavender whale flopped to the side of her dildo harness. At first I was embarrassed. Then I felt sad for her because she hadn't transformed me into a liberated sex machine like she said she could. Finally I felt angry. Erika and her friends really believed they'd invented hot sex and radical politics. Like, what did they think women had been doing for the last three billion years we've been on earth? Waiting for the 1990s when the sex radicals would show us how it's done?

I broke the silence saying, "I bet you're really thankful for the Catharine MacKinnons and Andrea Dworkins of this world. They keep sex good and dirty for you."

"Anti-sex prudes," Erika muttered, missing my point.

"I'm gonna whisper 'Catharine MacKinnon' in your ear while I fuck you and see what happens," I said.

Erika had a funny look on her face. She knew I was mocking her. Her ears reddened to match her lips.

"Erika," I said more gently now. "With all this apparatus in bed with us, I feel more like a lab animal than a woman having sex."

"Loosen up," she snapped. "You're just too uptight to allow yourself to feel good." She shifted her whole body into a pout.

"It seems to me that being able to get off without half a hardware store in the bed is more indicative of a 'looser' state of mind than needing all this crap. Believe me, my orgasms are superb with a hand or a mouth. What gets me off is the, oh, maybe you could say, essence of the other person. I don't need props. Come on, untie me and let me show you the old-fashioned way."

That sweet look of fear crossed Erika's face again.

"Come on, girlfriend. We've tried your way. Now try mine," I whispered. After Erika untied me, I swept all the gadgets onto the floor.

"Watch out!" she cried. "That stuff costs a lot of money."

"Sorry," I said quietly as I started to tongue her outer ear.

"You just have to control everything," she said, still petulant.

"Mmm, probably so," I said. I scooted down the bed to suck on her toes, one at a time. I reached a hand up under her ass and stroked the crack. I could feel all her muscles tense. I wondered if she felt too naked without her toys. I moved my mouth up her thigh and encountered the lavender whale. I used my teeth to undo her dildo harness. Each time she tried to help with her hands, I bit them. I heard her sigh a couple times. I didn't know if it was annoyance or the first stages of relaxing. Once I got the harness and dildo off her, I licked her clit ring, but not her clit. I circled around and around her labia, licking her thighs, stroking her anus, but not touching her clit. I wanted her to get so desperate she had to ask me.

She started moaning when I put a lubed finger up her anus. Then gasping as I put three fingers in her vagina. I moved the fingers, all four, in and out of her very, very slowly. She hauled her knees up as far as they would go and held them with her hands. Her head tossed back and forth and primeval sounds came from her throat.

Finally, she begged. "Oh god, Elizabeth, just do me

please." She even got my name right, for once. Still, I waited. I wouldn't touch her clit but I fucked her harder and faster with my fingers. She had to scream first. She had to scream before I'd touch her clit.

Then Erika did scream. "Oh please, oh please, oh please," she hollered. And I touched her clit lightly with the tip of my tongue, then sucked her until she came, wailing and bucking. The old-fashioned way.

Poems

GERRY GOMEZ PEARLBERG

Sailor

The girls go by in their sailor suits
They catch my eye in their sailor suits
Big or slight they all grin like brutes
In steam-ironed pants and buffed jet boots
They saunter right up my alley.

I study their easy, confident strides
Crews cuts and white hats capping decadent eyes
They shiver the pearl on night's oystery prize
They shiver me timbers, unbuckle me thighs
This alley was made for seething.

From the sweat of a street lamp or lap of the sea
A smooth sailor girl comes swimming to me
Says she wants it right now and she wants it for free
Clamps her palms to my shoulders, locks her knees to my
    knees
This alley was made for cruising.

Her face is dark coffee, her head has no hair
Her cap shines like neon in the bristling night air
She pins her brass metals to my black brassiere
Tucks her teeth like bright trophies behind my left ear
This alley is very rewarding.

She tosses her jacket and rolls up her sleeves
On her arm's a tattoo of an anchor at sea
She points to the anchor and whispers "That's me."
And the wetter I get the more clearly I see
This alley was made for submersion.

Her fingers unbutton my 501's
This girl's fishing for trouble and for troubling fun
She slides off her gold rings and they glint like the sun
Then she smirks, rubs her knuckles, and spits out her gum
This alley was made for swooning.

Now she's pushing her prow on my ocean's sponge wall
Uncorking my barnacle, breaking my fall
And there's pink champagne fizzling down my decks and
     my hall
As she wrecks her great ship on my bright port-of-call
This alley was made for drowning.

LESLÉA NEWMAN

Night on the Town

When I step into my red silk panties and swivel into
the matching strapless bra my butch bought me for
   Valentine's Day

When I slide on my black mesh stockings with toes pointed,
sitting on the edge of the bed like some Hollywood movie queen

When I shimmy into my spandex dress that sparkles and turns
over the tops of my thighs like a disco ball over a snappy crowd

When I puff on my pink clouds of blush, brush my eyelashes
long and lush, smear my lips and nails richer than ruby red

When I step into my sky high heels, snap on some shiny earrings
and slip seventeen silver bracelets halfway up my arm

When I dab my shoulders and neck, earlobes and wrists,
cleavage and thighs with thick, musky perfume

When I curl my hair into ringlets that dip over one eye
and bounce off my shoulder like a Clairol girl gone wild

When I turn from the mirror, pick up my purse
and announce to my butch that I'm ready to go

When I see her kick the door shut, hear her
declare, "We're not going anywhere tonight"

When I whine and say, "But we never go out,"
following her back to the bedroom, my lips in a pout

When I give in and let her have her way
with me pretending that wasn't my plan all along

CHEA VILLANUEVA

Butches

I'm a butch who digs femmes
makes no excuses for being top
A stone butch, cool butch, slow grinding butch
who feels sexy under a femme
BUTCH
in tuxedos, bad boy type
with an attitude
"Oh baby, let me do it to you, I can fuck you like no other."
A butch
who doesn't sleep with butches
butch
enough to rock a femme
all through the night
I'm a butch
who loves femmes
in the bed
on the floor
in the back seat of a car

I love a femme
who's all the woman she can be
who sits on my face
cums in my mouth
bites my ear
rides my cock
leaves scratches from my neck to my ass
screams my name like there's no ending

KYLA WAZANA

Offering

This is for you, butch lover with the blue eyes
This is for you
       with the blond hair and
       the white, white skin

For you I'll wait
Listening to your war stories
of street fights and
       cop encounters
East-end life and
       underground survival
Listen until the stone melts off the butch
       and some of your courage drips into me

For you I'll walk the edge of fear
Get on my knees and swallow it
in shadowy parks
and half-deserted streets
where only men meet

Give me your hand
and lead me
gentlemanly
behind the trees and the bushes
ride me
'til you're finished
and I'm not
I can wait

This is for you because you were called
"fag" and "white-trash"
And no-one knew that for years you were the girl
who cleaned up the vomit and the binges and the beatings
and the stale beer congealing
under packets of Export A
while as "jew" and "painted whore" I did the same

This is for you, butch lover
for the leather and the boots
for the shaved head
and the shit-kicker walk
through symbols
I wouldn't ever mistake on you
once I saw you smirk

For you and only you I'll play this dance of power
this dance of servitude
For you the slut-tight dresses and
pull-up stockings
the nails I'll never have to cut
cuz it's not my fingers you need:
at least not yet

And the garters that
snap against my thigh
just so hard
and the bites I let you leave on my
shoulders
because I want your bruises on me
before they even get there
I won't offer these to anyone else
although I might tease you with it

And fuck the safe space
cuz we both know there isn't one
This theory I learned at your feet:
there are only safe moments
in broken rules

OFFERING

PAMELA GRAY

San Diego

and you said   *how do you*
want it   slow or fast
and i said   *against*
the wall   and tease me
and you said   *stand up*
and you said   *turn around*
and i said   very little
and you said   *spread your legs*
and you said   *i'm gonna*
fuck you and you said
raise your arms   and you tied
my wrists with silk
and you said   *don't move*
and you slipped your hand
under my panties   and you said
don't move   and you slipped
your hand   under my teddy
your breath   on my neck   your mouth

on my shoulder   and then
the dildo   slipping
between my thighs   and you said
turn around   and you said
on your knees   and you said
make me hard   so i can fuck you
and you held   my head
as you moved   in and out
and you said   *on the bed*
and you went   inside me
and you went   deeper
and you said   *wrap your legs*
around me   and you said
wider   and you said
see   you finally got
your butch top
that's what femmes like you
really want   isn't it
and i said   *yes*
and i said   *yes*
and i said   *yes*

CHRISTINA STARR

i want

your legs open wide
lips slick with juice
    & clit ruby red

against my tongue
        my tongue
        will stroke it hard

i want your belly
    brave bare
    belly on my face

i want your breasts
    your ripe
    melon mounds
    in my mouth

i want your neck
    your tight
    brown skin
    coiled black hairs
        against my palm

i want your mouth
       i am thirsty
for your mouth
    craving the long
        wet swallow

i want my hand in your hair
        fisted   tight
    to hold on
      hold your head
        back

    with my fingers in

    force the pleasure
        out

  i want

    oh
  i want

    to make you   shout

CHRYSTOS

I Bought a New Red

dress to knock her socks off, spent all day looking for just
the right combination of sleeve & drape, so I could actually
knock all her clothes off   She met me at the boat dressed
so sharp she cut all the boys to ribbons

Over dinner in a very crowded queer restaurant I teased her
by having to catch drips of my food with my tongue, staring
into her eyes, daring her to lean over & grab my breast or
crotch & titillate the faggot waiters   She sat back soaking
me up, enjoying my teasing tidbits, for all the world not
wanting to fuck me ever   I knew better as she's kept me
on my back all night since we met   I began to pout because
I wasn't affecting her enough to suit me & she hadn't said
a thing about my dress   Just then the waiter brought our
dessert, a small cake she'd had decorated to say *Beg Me To
Fuck You*, with pink roses all around the edge

I laughed so hard I tore my dress a little   The waiter
smirked I fed her roses from the cake, she licked my fingers
so slowly I almost screamed   Near us some blazer dykes
were very nervous & offended, so naturally she began to
make loud sucking noises   Laughing, we left them to their
girl scout sex & went dancing, where she kept her hand on
my ass & her thigh between my legs even during the fast
ones   Going home she pulled my thigh-top stockings to my
knees & played with me   I'd worn no underpants especially for her   We were having such a good time she
couldn't park & we laughed as she tried a third time & I
blew in her ear almost causing a wreck

Then we started doing it in the front seat of her car, awkward with gear knob & wrong angles, until a cop pulled up
& said sarcastically through the open window   *Do you
need some assistance parking, Sir?*   She flamed as red as
my dress & returned to manoeuvring the car instead of me

I was so horny I could barely walk in my matching high
heels & she held my arm as we crossed to her place, pinching my nipple with her other hand & smiling her grin of
anticipation   We necked on the porch to upset her nosy
neighbours, who have twice complained about the noise I
made coming   Then she couldn't get the lock to work &
we giggled as I stood with heels in hand, my stockings full
of runs & a wet spot on the back of my silk dress almost as
wide as my ass   The door popped open so suddenly she
fell forward & I tumbled after her, gasping   I started up
the stairs heading for her bed when she caught hold of my
pubic hair with her hand & pulled me back onto her until I
was kneeling on the stairs as she tucked me from behind &
my dress ripped some more as she took me hard, kicking

the door shut with her foot, taking me out of this world until I was upside down with my head at the door & leg on the banister   Heat of her crotch as she came on me, my dress ripping right up the front as we laughed harder

The next morning her roommate said we were disgusting & we grinned with pride   The cleaners cannot repair the sweet dress & looked at me very oddly but I went out giggling & made her a pocket handkerchief with it, sewing rolled hems & a discreet message along one edge   *PLEASE rip my dress off anytime*

SHEILA WAHSQUONAIKEZHIK

Liquid Silk

Liquid silk
brown
gently
pours red fiery
desire through my veins

Black white hairs
baby fine
reveals her
womanly innocence

Her spirit
weaves
around my physical being
she envelopes the life of my soul

Locking
unlocking
chains of desire
linking
imaginations of unfulfilled fantasies

Twisting, turning
rushes of excitement
pumping through my body
her fingers
entering my domain

Inside
she dances to satisfy
my human need
for sexual
sensual pleasure

SANDRA HAAR

Eating a Mango

First, slice a line down the middle
Run your tongue along it
Lick up the juices
Peel back the outer skin
Bite greedily at the flesh inside
    (More juices will spurt out with each bite)
Suck hard to get it all,
    let it run over your bottom lip,
    drip off your chin,
    course a sticky line between your breasts,
    over your stomach —

ء

Kneel in front of her
Trace a line along the middle of her pussy
Run the hard tip of your tongue
    between the folds of her labia
Catch mango juice as it glides onto your tongue

MARY ANN MOORE

Eat Warm

Garlic changes its taste when baked long and slow
from sharpness to sweetness
then nutty when warm
>   Damp clove of woman
>   erect bud on my tongue
>   sweet in the melting
>   sharp as you peak

Whole heads of garlic
tops cut from each head
tight just like you are
before we undress
>   I rub your bare back
with butter, olive oil, a sprinkle of thyme
>   No need for an oven
>   the heat is inside
>   roasting under cover

exposing to baste
>   the cloves protrude when they're swelling
>   your clitoris swims

Drip onto me
mingle your juices with mine
heat me don't melt me
I want you to come first

        Your thighs glisten with moisture
        the sheets warmed underneath
        you play all around it
        teasing with glee
        panting with pleasure
        I'm turning you on
        my body's reaction
        and what your tongue does to me

The recipe book page is stained
with butter and oil
My sheets are scented with lavender and you
damp in some spots

        wetter in others
        Orgasmic pleasure
        delight in the tongue
        lips swollen with the pleasure
        of your taste in me

Eat me for dinner
bake long and slow
garnish with laughter

        understanding you know

Your smell on my fingers
Garlic on my tongue
long after lingering

        smells in the air

Squeeze garlic cloves on top
eat warm

CAROL CAMPER

Camellia

Wishing wanting
garden nect'ry bower for bed
holding glory hips abound beneath my arm
around arching back she blooms
Liquid looks in torrents eye to eye
connect two rushing falling see I see
lip corners gentle nudge to smile
Leaping touching
loving heart for hand... here... have
Slippery silken cheek to lip
and berry arcing wetly wetly
Moving rolling ride
never quell I her storm inside
Hot petal deeply edged in
black tiny bud boil quiver
Lips stretch screaming silent anthem
hearts to hear and then
escape through crystal vibrant sound

SHEILA WAHSQUONAIKEZHIK

Leaves

Sensuous leaves
Turn brilliant colours.
Dew drops form
Wet, sweet.
Wind whispers Sky's desire.
Sun warms
Filling air
With loving heat.
Rains fall
Clearing old hurts.
Where is Night-time Peace?
Wrapped in arms of Morning Sun.
Water caresses
Liquid Silk.
Champagne Hope
Arches rainbow colours.
Reaching for
Wisps of grass.

TARA HART

autoerotic

she lifts the
hood plunging
fingers in circles
oily shafts
drenching her
hands in earth warm
ooze
leaning in
her thighs ride
the gaping fenders
in an ardent grip

turn her on she yells
as the engine moans
and sighs she turns
a loving ear to the
churning chaos
knowing just

what to do
to make it
turn over

oil soaked denim
stretches over her
active limbs as she
probes and worries
the suspected parts

she wants to up
my idling speed

regular maintenance
will cut down
on wear

being serviced
provides such
relief

Lois Fine

Sex for Dyke Mothers

You send me a package
a plain brown wrapper from a sex shop in San Francisco
I open it after a day at the office
in transit from daycare in freezing rain
sit on the couch before supper and feel it

It comes with instructions
"Take your time. Go slowly."
What if I only have after supper
bathtime storytime bedtime until morning
then breakfast and getting-dressed time?
Going slow may not be an option

Tearing lettuce I think of your gift
my lover and I try it later
don't bother with candles, the bath,
music, foreplay, too many kisses
Just hurry and try it like a game

instead of tv
Finish before our eyes close
careful not to leave it on our bedside table

Mornings come early at our place

LAURA IRENE WAYNE

A Womyn's Touch

approach me with love
sweet aromatic love
touch me
stroke me
with your burnt desire
make my body ache
cry for your touch
move without hesitation
and let the hunger of your tongue
seek the sweetness of my body
allow it to explore among the dulcet
petals of my labia
so you and I can enjoy the hardness
of my awaiting clit
let the hot wetness of your tongue
shower my secret petals with love
allow it to sample the nectar
so you and I together can share
the secrets of blossoming
under a womyn's touch

NICOLE TANGUAY

In the Here and Now

For all my Two-Spirited sisters.
I want you in the here and now
like days gone by
when the smell of your body awakened my senses
and good food was common place
I want you in the here and now
when memories were present
nothing stood between us
except our own fears
of intimacy
I want you in the here and now
when I could feel your wetness
against my thigh
the taste of you lingering
on my lips
when just being together
was enough
I want you in the here and now
when summer was at her finest

and the rest of the world
did not exist
I want you in the here and now
beside me

JOCHEW

Love Lies

you burst into my life
took my heart, reshaped it
i was an angel made flesh
...in your eyes
the Queen of Pentacles
always in your Tarot

was i an illusion?
a fantasy?

then you left... "I need to be alone,
I'm sorry..."
no explanation, no invitation
to talk

i was mislead, you lied
i was set up, you weren't honest
a dagger in my heart, stab deeply

rip it to shreds
can't mend, not now

this barrier of silence prevails
passionate memories blend with emptiness
sweet contours...
still,
as vivid as the first morning
awakened

writing feverishly, damn you
desperate to purge you
writing dangerously in defiance of your silence and
unkind words
i respected you and left you alone
just two months and you're with someone new

haunting memories of ecstasy
we shared each day
your scent on my fingers
taste and feel you
still,
your urgent cries echo
still,
next to me in the darkness
i long for the feel of
your breath on my skin
your lips sliding across mine
your tongue dancing within
and you inside me
again

your continual silence destroys me
now your love lies with her
you said our love was growing
and you need me
where did it grow to?

FRANCES YIP HOI

Orchestrated Sounds of Seduction

Your heels walk hitting high pitch against the concrete
cars rush by
wind-tunnels travel forward and backward
inside and outside my space
kissing deep throat against my neck
to bury my face deep inside your breast
holding me tight
until I see your face for the first time in hours

Your gladiator rubberwear
fastened tight along the length of my chest
your body in its tightness
holds fast in orchestration
where each stroke of your cat-o'-nine tails
strikes hard against my open legs
my stomach rises to reach your jewelled cunt

My tongue finds your clit ring
as you sit across my face
I probe inside you
with lips thick and thirsting
as your hands beat fast against my thighs
my nose is buried deep under your skin

Lasting for hours extending in a conflation of sounds
stilettos hitting hard with a high pitch in the busy city street
your hands moving rhythmically against my thighs
your teeth suck hard in allegro against my pink pussy
each suck breaks into the silence
and I imagine that your crescendo increases with heavy
    breathing

You come out wet against my beaten thigh
you inner muscles working hard
nearly precise
mechanical
almost calculated
cloudbursting with rain against my thirsting skin
whips cracking like thunder across the sky
your voice resonates inside my mind again

To Coda
Fingers moving along the length of my opening
striking hard against its wetness
heat reaching deep
touching skin
engorged and swollen
with resonance coming out like ripples
as sound waves in my wetness
Fini

JACQUIE BISHOP

Midnight Air

I cleanse my body of the day
  oils sheen it moonlight makes it glow
My hair drips water from the city's pipes
  the room fills with midnight air
Lightly I wrap the towel 'round me
as I make way to my bed
There I touch   caress
  my thighs
   breasts
   hands
Hands work their way up to   onto   into me
  The feel of hair the smell of heat
My hair   heat
  I sweat as my insides swell
Hips thrust   ass tightens
  Fingers tug and play with me mine slowly
First one then two all the time
  wanting more — of me

MARY FRANCES PLATT

Oxygenated Babe

Now that I'm using oxygen
I imagine you won't desire me
tube wrapped round breast covering mound belly
over full thighs down long strong foot
trailing over bedclothes sleeze-clothes cunts
wrapping cinching full behind

Now that I'm using oxygen
You probably won't want me
to remove the cannula from my nose
wet your nipple
play tunes with continuous
cool pure air
lick your pussy and share breath
one for me one for you
You probably wouldn't be interested
in hearing a longer louder come
from a stronger safer heart

Now that I'm using oxygen
I imagine you're no longer interested
in spanking mountainous buttocks
renewed sighs of pleasure
moans of release
wrapped in spiralling tubing incandescence
I imagine you wouldn't delight in knowing
lungs are safe for piercing screams
from probing fist
Up and down in and out
now joy and not no breath
which is different than
Oh Baby you leave me breathless or
Sweetheart the sight of you in those tight jeans
takes my breath away

Now that I'm using oxygen
I'd delight in being used
to fulfill any oxygenated babe fantasies
that might be swimming around that
nasty little head of yours
The same head
that refuses to equate severely disabled
with Honey you couldn't possibly make me wet
Cuz I do, and we are, hot for each other

Now that I'm using oxygen
I know I'm still alive feel your touch, touch you
want your body your body wants me
hands tongues cunt-hairs entwined
amidst umbilical cord life-sustaining rhythms

ELLEN WARWICK

Her Rough Hands

her rough hands
move down her torso
and back up again
she is touching herself
as i touch her
she doesn't know
that her hands
on her body
are making me ready to cum

watching her in the half-light
she is part of me
and i her
we are the embodiment of connection
i tell her in my mind to touch me
there
and there
she does

no distinction between spoken words
and the desires burning through my head
one touch and i cum
crying in her ear
grabbing her flesh
wanting to pull her into me
no longer two bodies pleasing each other
but one woman's body pleasing itself

For Jen

MARY FRANCES PLATT

Strong Hands

Strong hands
assured, knowing they can sustain oneself
take what they want
give pleasure as desired

Strong hands
teasing, lying quietly by your side
making promises of passion to come

Strong hands
feeling, touching, stroking, pulling
creating ecstasy in movement slow, fast, gentle, rough

Strong hands
eagerly riding orgasms' waves
meeting each crest with passion and force

Strong hands
resting again
nurturing, quieting, comforting, whispering endearments

Strong hands
Strong hands of a lover
Strong hands of a lover living with cancer

Jacquie Buncel

Anatomy of Love

hands,
I watched you gesture in meetings
across the boardroom table
convey your point with passion and belief
now you tenderly
stroke cheeks, closed eyelids, ear lobes
gently glide over inner thighs

fingers,
I praised your skill
as you deftly secured a canoe to the top of a car
pulled ropes
tied firm knots
now you move in and out between my fingers
caress my nipples
play with knots in my clit hair

legs,
I admired your strength
as you pushed the canoe from the shore
crawled over knapsacks to your seat
now you intertwine with my legs
my foundation as I rock on top of you
I build and build

breasts,
I noticed your gentle curves
under pink silk shirts
turtle-neck jerseys and purple sweatshirts
so many layers
now you rhythmically rub against me
I tease you
envelop you in my mouth
suck you like heavenly liquid
I can't waste a drop

vulva,
I didn't allow myself to think of you
nestled
in jeans, sweat pants, long underwear
now I circle your contours
finger your wetness

face,
I knew all your expressions
eyes lengthening in kindness
disbelieving lift of one eyebrow
now I see tiny lines beside your nose
when you smile
you crinkle like crumpled clothes

eyes shut
you concentrate, turn inward
as sensation grows

mouth,
I knew your words, your tone
before
you spoke in public
so much self-assurance
you instructed me
paddle into the waves
and *this is how to tie a reef knot*
now you say
sweetie, girlfriend, gorgeous
demand
suck me
whisper
you are so sexy

woman,
is it any wonder
I am surprised
discovering you
my colleague, my friend
now
my lover

Rozie

Confessions

I like

to be taken
before the crack of dawn

fingers prying my soft folds
insisting
spreading my languid legs out wide

gentle hands brushing against my sleepy flesh
long fingers
pushing
hotly sweetly

yielding
my body surrenders wet
my woman smell
rising
filling our love chamber

lover's early morning heat
burn into my skin
deep thrusts
piercing my centre

passion concealed under night's weight
engulf me

between crumpled sheets
my dreams transform
in predawn stillness

I like

the advent of a new day's sounds of lust
primitive rhythms of flesh
bruising my skin
engulfing my senses

my body
indolent
rises to meet lover's crystalline need

morning rider leaves me
groaning
in ecstasy

I like
to listen to my sweet rider
coming
between murmurs of hello

CHRISTINA MILLS

What I Did When I Got Home

took in the morning paper
turned off the porch light
remembered our first kiss
(dance, date, night together)
drank some orange juice
read my horoscope
read your horoscope
thought of twenty-three ways to insert the phrase "my
    lover" into a conversation
turned down the thermostat
remembered your heat
(softness, strength, wetness)
undressed
remembered your hands
put on my night-gown
remembered your breasts
washed my face
remembered your face vivid with pleasure

brushed my teeth
breathed your scent on my fingers
carefully avoided washing my left hand
crawled into bed
breathed your scent on my fingers
turned out the light
curled up on my side
breathed your scent on my fingers
rested my hand on the pillow close to my face
fell asleep

smiling

CHRYSTOS

Hold Me Down

tie me to my bed with silk so I can't get away
since I don't want
to anyway
Pull my skirt over my head
face lost in hot ruffles
Fuck me with your strap on
'til my pussy sucks
Screaming to let me free I want you
to hold me there in that sharp gasping
before exploding
Grab my hair & wrap it around your fist
growling
make me come
when I beg you to stop
I'm ready to go
over
Make me

Contributors

Jacquie Bishop is a Black lesbian poet and feature writer, living in her native Brooklyn, NY. She is the founder and artistic director of MAMA DOESN'T KNOW! Productions, and an AIDS and Women's Healthcare and Sex/Sexuality educator. Her creative works have appeared in *On Our Backs, Bad Attitudes, We Be Wimmin's Press, Womanews, Black Leather In Color, BLK, Lambda Book Report, Lesbians on Love* and many other gay and progressive papers and magazines. She has also performed her works throughout the Unites States. She is presently seeking a publisher for her manuscript of poetry *Thinking Out Loud*, and is working on a series of short stories entitled *Tea, Toast and Medicine*.

Lucy Jane Bledsoe's *Sweat: Stories and a Novella* (Seal Press) and children's book, *The Big Bike Race* (Holiday House), will both be published in the fall of 1995. She has edited a lesbian erotica anthology called *Hot Licks: Stories of Lesbian Longing* (Alyson), also coming out in the fall of 1995.

Beth Brant is a Bay of Quinte Mohawk from Tyendinaga Mohawk Territory in Ontario. She is the editor of *A Gathering of Spirit*, the ground-breaking collection of writing and art by Native women and of *in a vast dreaming*, the first issue of *Native Women in the Arts*. She is the author of *Mohawk Trail*, prose and poetry, *Food & Spirits*, short fiction and *Writing as Witness*, a collection of essays. Brant is currently working on a book of Tyendinaga Elders' oral histories, *I'll Sing Til the Day I Die* and a book of essays about Land and Spirit entitled *Testimony from the Faithful*. She is a mother and grandmother and lives with her partner of eighteen years, Denise Dorsz. She has been writing since the age of forty and considers it a gift for her community.

Joannie Brennan was told to write about what she knows. That'd be sex.

Jacquie Buncel is a Jewish lesbian writer and activist. She lives in Toronto with her cat Harvey (Milk). She has been involved in the labour, disability and feminist movements and has worked with other Jewish women in support of a Palestinian homeland. She currently works on anti-poverty and housing issues. She is an active member of Women's Press and appreciates the encouragement and support of the wonderful staff at the Press. Her writing has been published in the *Jewish Women's Issue* of *Fireweed* and in *Out Rage: Dykes and BIs Resist Homophobia*.

Carol Camper is a writer, editor and visual artist. Born in Toronto and raised in southwestern Ontario, she is a Black woman whose racial ancestry also includes Native North American and European. Carol's writing appears in numerous anthologies and periodicals, including *Fireweed*, *Canadian Woman Studies* and *Piece of My Heart: A Lesbian of Colour Anthology*. Carol's most recent project, the anthology, *Miscegenation Blues: Voices of Mixed Race Women* was released by Sister Vision Press in 1994 and is in its second printing.

Chrystos was born November 7, 1946, off reservation, to a Meniminee father and a Lithunian/Alsace-Lorraine mother. She is a self-educated artist and writer, and an activist for numerous Native Rights & Prisoners' causes. She is author of the books *Not Vanishing* (1988), *Dream On* (1991), *In Her I Am* (1993), *Fugitive Colors* (1994) and the forthcoming *Fire Power*.

Catherine Creede lives in Toronto where she works among people who would be shocked. This is her first published work of fiction.

Deb Ellis: I live in Dunnville, Ontario, work at Margaret Frazer House in Toronto, and do political work with the Alliance for Non-Violent Action and other groups.

Rosamund Elwin has been involved in publishing for the past eight years, working on children's and adults' books. Her involvement in publishing children's books sparked her interest in writing for children. This led to the co-written stories *Asha's Mums* and *The Moonlight Hide & Seek Club*. Rosamund sees publishing first-time writers as cultural activism. She enjoys publishing and wants to see many more of her ideas materialise, including anthologies on lesbians and men, and Caribbean lesbians, both of which she is currently developing.

Lois Fine: I am a double chai double scorpio cruising through the streets of Toronto with Barney songs in my head.

Ellen R. Flanders is a (Toronto/Montreal/Jerusalem) Jewish dyke photographer and activist living in New York. Her work has appeared in *Fireweed, Rites, Xtra!, Borderlines* and *The Girl Wants To*. She is teaching and pursuing an MFA at Rutgers University, and attending the Whitney Museum Independent Studio Program. Ellen is currently producing a series of photos called "Lacking Desire," dealing with the construction of (hetero)gendered sexuality.

Pamela Gray, born 1956 in Brooklyn, is a Jewish lesbian poet, playwright and screenwriter living in Santa Monica. She is the author of a poetry chapbook, *the lesbian breakup manual,* and her work appears in many anthologies, including *The Femme Mystique, Sleeping with Dionysus* and *Cats and Their Dykes*. Pamela won the 1993 Woman in the Moon poetry prize and is writing the screenplay adaption of *Stone Butch Blues*.

Sandra Haar is co-ordinating editor of a feminist journal. She also teaches sunday school at a secular Jewish community centre. Her writing and artwork have been published in *Canadian Woman Studies, Centre/fold, Fuse, Fireweed, Matriart, Rites, Xtra!, Vanguard,* as well as the anthology *The Girl Wants To* (Coach House Press). Sandra has been producing sexually explicit art for ten years. Born in Montreal in 1967; Pisces with Scorpio rising and Cancer moon. "All For You" also forms part of an image/text work in progress. "Eating a Mango" was written late one summer night.

Eve Harris is the pseudonym of a New York City girl who divides her time between writing and loitering in nightclubs.

tara hart is an art instructor who lives and works in the Toronto area. She believes that lesbian literature adds an essential dimension to the community by providing images that affirm our lives. Writing poetry and short stories has allowed her to give expression to her thoughts and feelings as well as entertain her lesbian friends. Her work has been featured in *Matriart* magazine and local newspapers. tara is grateful for this opportunity to join hearts and minds with all of you.

Frances Yip Hoi is a collector of Queer "lures" ranging from fish bait hooks to fish shaped nail clippers. As a transgendered, mixed-race individual, she enjoys androgyny and passing. She uses mixed media to explore the tactile relationship of imagination, desire and identity. She has written "Cleaning out the Closet in Grandma's Home" in *At the Crossroads: Journal for Women of African Descent*, and is satiated by publicizing lesbian lust. She is a Women's Studies student at the University of Toronto.

jochew, a lesbian of Chinese descent living in Toronto, has been writing in seclusion since the age of 7 on scattered bits of paper and shoving them into a folder under her dusty, cat hair-covered bed. Labelled a reluctant writer by friends and co-workers, this is her first published piece. This poem was prompted by a recent painful breakup with a partner whom she truly and deeply cared for and loved. This piece is her own proper closure to that event. She plans to continue writing if the mood arises again.

Kiss & Tell is a collective of three lesbian artists, Persimmon Blackbridge, Lizard Jones and Susan Stewart, in Vancouver, Canada who have been working together for more than nine years on issues of sexuality and representation. They have created and performed several explicit sexual works, including *Drawing The Line*, an interactive photo exhibit, and *True Inversions*, a multi-media performance.

C. Allyson Lee: There are only two things that will get me up out of bed: guitars just waiting to be stroked and Warriors with butchy overhanded throws. Look for me in *Pearls of Passion* (co-editor), *The Other Woman*, *Out Rage*, *The Very Inside*, *Piece of My Heart* and say HI.

April Miller is a fat, bi-racial, high femme S/M dyke who lives, works and performs in the San Francisco Bay area. She is a member of the editorial collective of *FaT GiRL* magazine and a former member of Fat Lips Readers Theater (for whom "Butch Baiting" was written). Her work has appeared in *FaT GiRL*, *Venus Infers* and the book *Woman En Large: Images of Fat Nudes*.

Christina Mills (A.K.A. Army Brat, A.K.A. Bookworm, A.K.A. Four-eyes, A.K.A. Aw, *Mo*-om, A.K.A. *May I Help You, Sir?*, A.K.A. *gringa*, A.K.A. Auntie Chris, A.K.A. No. 2 in Her Age Group — in a field of 2, A.K.A. Uppity Dyke, A.K.A. *la mujer araña*, A.K.A. Hairless Two-Legs Can't Catch A Mouse & Always Late with Dinner, A.K.A. Cranberry Bogg) always answers to Love. She lives on a hill in the Gatineau.

Mary Ann Moore is a white lesbian, of Irish and German descent, and a mother of two, living and writing in Toronto. She received a Canada Council Explorations grant to work on her first novel, *Ordinary Life*, in which the protagonist, a lesbian playwright, uncovers homophobia and racism in her search for heroines in the unravelling of her own story.

Joan Nestle is a fifty-four-year-old Jewish femme who never tires of drawing the pictures of desire. She is a co-founder of the Lesbian Herstory Archives, author of *A Restricted Country* (Firebrand Books, 1988) and editor of *The Persistent Desire: A Fem-Butch Reader* (Alyson Publications, 1991).

Lesléa Newman is an author and editor with twenty books to her credit including *The Femme Mystique, Sweet Dark Places, Love Me Like You Mean It, Every Woman's Dream* and *Heather Has Two Mommies*. She is currently editing a big, fat collection of contemporary lesbian love poems due out from Ballantine Books in 1996.

Gerry Gomez Pearlberg's fiction and poetry have appeared in numerous publications, including *Calyx, Global City Review, modern words* and *Sister and Brother: Lesbians and Gay Men Write about Their Lives Together*, edited by Joan Nestle and John Preston. She has edited *The Key To Everything: Classic Lesbian Love Poems* (St. Martin's Press), and is currently editing an anthology of erotic lesbian verse. She lives in Brooklyn with Otto, her beloved boxer muse.

Mary Frances Platt is, according to her girlfriend, a fat sexy crip activist who likes to keep busy creating accessible integrated crip and non crip culture. She is a loud mouthed biculturally raised (poor white trash and working class; french-canadian-american and irish-american) femme who is not known for her docility, but is known for her great tits.

Claire Robson: I am a forty-one year old lesbian, born and schooled in England. I resigned my vice-principal's job seven years ago, because the price I paid in fear and compromise about my self and my sexuality was too high, and because I wanted to be a writer and be free. My lover and best friend, Joy, wanted to study in the States so we cast our bread on the waters and came, sight unseen. We now run a small woman-identified commercial window cleaning business, and spend the rest of our time creatively. I try to write the truth, which isn't always tidy or pleasant. When I saw my parents die, I realised that life is too short to tell lies and do things I don't believe in, and that's what I try to live now.

Stephanie Rosenbaum is a San Francisco journalist, writer and spoken-word performer. The first chapter of *Angelina*, her upcoming mystery novel, was recently published in *Beyond Definition: New Lesbian and Gay Writing from San Francisco*. She likes to write about food, clothes and sex, and is currently working as a restaurant reviewer and fashion critic for the *San Francisco Bay Guardian*.

Rozie is a hot cool babe.

christina starr is a writer, editor, activist and mother living in downtown Toronto. Her work includes critical essays, poetry, short fiction, and her first poetic monologue for the stage, *holding...*, was produced at the 1994 Edmonton Fringe Festival. Her inspiration, in writing and in life, comes most often from her daughter, from women, sexual intensity and lesbian reality.

Judith P. Stelboum is Associate Professor of Literature and Women's Studies at the College of Staten Island of City University of New York. She has had fiction, poetry and essays published in *Common Lives/Lesbian Lives* and in *Sinister Wisdom*, and is a reviewer for the *Lesbian Review of Books*. Recent work appears in the anthologies *Sister and Brother, Resist! Essays Against a Homophobic Culture, Not the Only One* and *Hot Licks*.

Nicole Tanguay is of French and Cree heritage. After living in B.C. most of her life, she now resides in Toronto. She is a Two-Spirited poet, musician and political activist. She has been in a number of anthologies including *Sweet Grass Road, Miscegenation Blues, Out Rage: Lesbian and BIs Resist Homophobia*. She believes in the voice of the Nishnawbe peoples and that is what gives her strength to continue to do the work that she does.

Karen X. Tulchinsky is a Jewish lesbian writer who lives in Vancouver. Her work has appeared in numerous anthologies including *Sister and Brother, Afterglow* and *The Femme Mystique*. She is the co-editor of *Queer View Mirror*, an anthology of gay and lesbian short, short fiction. Her first collection of short stories, *In Her Nature*, will be published by Women's Press in the fall of 1995.

Chea Villanueva likes to write about butch/femme relationships and everything pertaining to lesbians of color. She is the author of *Jessie's Song* and lives in the queer ghetto of San Francisco.

Sheila Wahsquonaikezhik is a 2-Spirited Anishnawbe Kwe from Rankin Reserve 15D in Sault Ste. Marie, Ontario. She currently works as the Palliative Care Project Coordinator at 2-Spirited People of the 1st Nations in Toronto. Also, Sheila is working on completing her autobiography which she hopes will be finished by the fall of 1995. She says that a large part of her writing facilitates her own journey of both personal and cultural reclamation work. She is inspired and encouraged to conitnue writing by reading the words and hearing the voices of other First Nation woman writers. Meegwetch to all who have paved the way for emerging women writers.

Ellen Warwick: I am a young urban dyke, struggling through English at the University of Toronto, hoping to eventually earn more than minimum wage. This is the first time I've been brave enough to submit a piece of myself.

Laura Irene Wayne is an African American Lesbian painter, printmaker, poet, graphic artist and writer. For the past thirteen years she has exhibited locally, nationally and internationally. Her work has appeared in and on the covers of magazines, books, journals and newspapers and can be found in private collections in Japan, London, Toronto, New York, Chicago and Atlanta. Her first book, *Journey To Feel* is now available.

Kyla Wazana is a North African Jewish woman living in Toronto. Presently finishing her B.A. in English literature, she aims to pursue a career that will take her straight to the top of any well-paying hierarchy. *Offering* is dedicated to Cawthra Park, a gay men's cruise park in Toronto, and was written to explore issues of power, sex and race, and how these issues interconnect with butch/femme roles. Kyla tries not to wear any natural fibre clothing.

Jess Wells is the author of the novel *AfterShocks* (Third Side Press, U.S./The Women's Press, U.K.). Wells has also published two volumes of short stories *Two Willow Chairs* (short fiction), *The Dress/The Sharda Stories* (short fiction and erotica) and has had work appear in thirteen literary anthologies within the lesbian, gay and women's movement. Her work "The Dress" was the first piece to herald the new discovery of femme-drag; her stories "The Succubus" and "Morning Girls" are cited as among the earliest of lesbian erotica; her story "Two Willow Chairs," frequently reprinted, is now included in university curricula and textbooks. She resides in the San Francisco Bay area.

Jana Williams is a working-class writer, who organized the Gay Games Literary Festival held in Vancouver in August of 1990. She is the author of the novel *Scuttlebutt* and is currently at work on a screenplay for a feature-length film.

Rosamund Elwin and Karen X. Tulchinsky

Photo: Dianne Whelan